SHOWDOWN!

"Get him!" someone shouted from behind him. Holden jumped as the helicopter slipped right, his fists tightening on the support struts along the underside of the craft. Pistol shots rang out from below him. Holden's body jerked as he felt something tear at his right foot. His left hand slipped from its purchase. He realized he was losing his grip.

He looked up, his eyes squinted against the downdraft. Through the open fuselage door, he could see Rosie. She was trussed up on the floor, gagged, her skirts up to her hips, her feet kicking wildly toward Borsoi. There was a gun in Borsoi's hand.

Borsoi kicked Rosie. Her body collapsed in a heap beside the plush-covered passenger bench. Then he turned toward the open door, a look in his eyes like nothing Holden had ever seen, like nothing human . . .

Other titles in the Defender series:

DECISION TIME

Jerry Ahern

A DELL BOOK

*This one's for Bill Craig,
an old friend and reader—
all the best . . .*

Published by
Dell Publishing
a division of
Bantam Doubleday Dell
Publishing Group, Inc.
666 Fifth Avenue
New York, New York 10103

ISBN: 0-440-20102-0

Printed in the United States of America
Published simultaneously in Canada

January 1989

10 9 8 7 6 5 4 3 2 1

KRI

CHAPTER 1

It was a different sort of thumping noise than the air conditioner made sometimes. And the dishwasher would have shut off hours ago.

Ellie Shorter pulled the sheet up under her chin as she sat up. Her nightgown was twisted around her and was up past her waist and she was suddenly cold all over. Her upper arms goose-pimpled as she hugged them across her chest. "There's somebody in the house, Scott."

Ellie Shorter felt like "Blondie" in the comic strips (she wished she looked like her) when she would hear a strange noise downstairs and try awakening her husband. Maybe she empathized with the durably curvaceous blonde because their husbands reacted in much the same manner. "Go back to sleep, Ellie," he told her. Not that she'd done it that often over the fourteen years they'd been married, tried to wake him up after a hard day at the office because she'd heard some unidentifiable noise in the night. Each time, after finally getting him to go downstairs and look, there had been nothing, of course, and she'd felt foolish afterward but happy because she was safe in her home, safe with her children. Scott didn't believe in owning a gun (her father had taught her how to shoot before she was ten and she'd grown up with guns in the house). But what would they do if there actually was someone in the house and all Scott had to defend the family with was a softball bat? She tried not to think about that, half tempted now to just roll over and tell herself the noise she'd heard was just her imagination or one too many cups of coffee.

But Ellie Shorter heard the noise again. She'd rather have the VCR and her grandmother's silver tea set stolen than have Scott walk down into something dangerous. But if the intruder wasn't just a thief, was after something more disgusting . . . There were home-invasion horror stories in the newspapers all the time, analyses of the motivations behind such nauseatingly violent crimes ranging from suppressed sexual urges to pure and simple sadism to just blind rage against society. "Scotty! Wake up. Scotty? Please?" She rested the soles of her feet—cold—against the small of his back.

His body twitched and he rolled over. "I'm awake, all right? How the hell could anybody sleep? What's wrong?"

"I hear something."

"What?"

"Somebody's in the house!"

"It's one of the kids going to the bathroom. Go to sleep."

"No—I mean, it's not Tommy or Meghan. The noise is downstairs, Scotty."

"Shit, honey. You know what time it is?"

She'd been watching the clock on and off for the last five minutes. "It's four-thirteen in the morning."

"Burglars don't get up that early. I gotta go to work in three hours, huh? I was at the judge-of-elections meeting until nine-thirty last night and I'm tired! Come on, huh? Lemme go to sleep."

Then she heard the noise again, and when she looked at Scott in the half-light—there was a nearly full moon and it had been hot and clear and she could see his face clearly—when she looked at him she saw in the corners around his eyes that he'd heard the noise too. It wasn't the air conditioner thumping, wasn't anything normal-sounding at all.

He was up, out of bed, reaching for his robe. After fourteen years of marriage she still couldn't get it out of her head that grown men looked silly naked. "Call 911 and tell them you suspect we have a prowler. Tell them I'm going downstairs to check it out. And, for God's sake, tell the police I don't own a damn gun so they don't come in shooting."

"I wish we did—own one."

"Right-wing psychos like the Patriots own guns, not normal people."

She'd argued with him over and over again years ago, finally given up, always kept the Chinese cleaver sharp and available when he was away overnight, wished he would change his mind—even a .22 would have been something. "The children?"

"I'll wake them up and send them back here to stay with you. It's—ah—it's probably nothing, okay?" She thought his voice lacked conviction.

Scott took the softball bat out of the closet. In her nightgown, not taking the time for a robe, she was already through tapping out the touch tones for the emergency number. A busy signal. She hung up, tried again. Another busy.

Scott was stepping out into the hallway. She dialed the operator, calling after Scott in a stage whisper, "Be careful!" The operator came on the line. "Operator. I need the police. It's an emergency. I'm at—"

"For police, fire, or medical emergencies, dial 911."

"I tried dialing 911, Operator. All I get is a busy signal."

"If you'd like, I can try dialing for you."

"Yes—but—" The operator was dialing already.

"Mommie?" It was Meghan, her nine-year-old voice sounding dry and tired, her little hands balled into fists and rubbing against her half-closed eyes.

There was another busy signal. "That number is busy," the operator said emotionlessly.

"It can't be busy!" Ellie Shorter realized she was sounding hysterical. "It—"

"If you think there may be trouble on the line, I can give you the number of Repair Service or I can dial it for you so you can re—"

Ellie hung up, slamming the receiver down so loudly, she thought she'd awaken the dead.

Tommy, twelve, wore only pajama bottoms and was barefoot. His reed-thin upper body rippled with awakening muscles. He sat down on the edge of the bed, pulling their sheet around him. Ellie dialed 911 again, herself. It was ringing. It was answered: ". . . in sequence. You have reached 911 for—"

"Thank God—somebody's—" And she felt a sick feeling suddenly wrenching at her stomach. She was talking to a recording. She hugged Tommy to her. Meghan plopped down onto the floor beside the bed and rested her head against Ellie's right thigh.

". . . will be answered by the next available operator. Do not hang up. All calls are answered in sequence. You have reached 911—" And the line went dead, totally dead. Maybe it was some strange kind of holding system? If she hung up and tried again, she'd lose her place, though, and maybe she wouldn't even get through again.

She looked at the bedroom door. She dropped the telephone.

"You lose this, bitch?"

A man—he was only a tall boy, maybe a half dozen years older than Tommy. And there were two other man-boys standing behind him. She sucked in her breath and bunched what remained of the sheet around her—why hadn't she put on her robe? Tommy's body tensed beside her. Meghan started breathing hard. Was Meghan having one of her asthma attacks? Lose what? Then Ellie Shorter's eyes tracked from the man-boy's pimple-splotched face to his hands. In his right he held a knife and blood dripped from it. In his left he held Scott's softball bat. "I asked you a fuckin' question, bitch! You lose the damn bat the hero was playin' with?"

"No!" Ellie exhaled the word without intending to speak.

Meghan shrieked and Tommy tried standing up. The softball bat crashed downward toward Tommy's head. Another man-boy dragged Meghan toward him, ripping away her nightgown. The bat hit Tommy's head and there was a cracking sound that made Ellie Shorter vomit. She screamed and started to choke and Tommy was dead on the bed beside her. One of the man-boys was touching Meghan's bare body with his filthy hands and the blood-dripping knife was plunging down as Ellie Shorter tried to grab little Meghan away and . . .

CHAPTER 2

Holden's Rolex Sea-Dweller's luminous black face read 4:36 A.M., his eyes shifting to it for an instant as he glanced over the lip of the wall. Four men in dark clothing, carrying assault rifles, were all he'd counted. But, according to Luther Steel, there should be six security men on duty at all times. Holden's SEAL training had covered clandestine penetrations, but never black-bag jobs. And this was one of those. He was up, moving in a low, crouching run. As he looked back along the wall, Rosie Shepherd was slightly behind him. And behind her tagged Scapalini, carrying his black backpack rather than wearing it.

Holden had asked Rosie Shepherd to stay at the camp, her left bicep still bandaged from the gunshot wound she had sustained in New Mexico. But he knew he was using her wound as an excuse, something she would never do. Granted, it was only a grazing wound and had bled itself clean. Tetanus and antibiotic shots were administered almost immediately and there was no sign of infection, the bandage merely to protect the wound while her body completed the healing process. But, he had to admit, he was happy she was backing him up. She was the best fighter he had—among other things. He had tried using her wound as an excuse to keep her out of danger. And keeping Rosie Shepherd out of danger was almost impossible unless he married her and they changed their names and moved out of the country. He had the money for that, to start over with a new life.

But what about the old life?

Without trying to, David Holden had become the leader of one of the largest and decidedly the most effective of the Patriot cells that were taking shape everywhere throughout the United States. Most of the Patriot cells were run by well-intentioned men who knew nothing of waging a war of counterinsurgency. Many of the Patriot cells were little more than armed debating societies that wrote letters to newspapers and television stations and postered slogans on alley walls. Some of them fought, but few fought all that well.

The Patriots, comprised mostly of veterans or police officers, but drawing in smaller percentages from literally all walks of life (he wondered absently as he ran along the wall's length if there were any more college professors like himself), had pitted themselves against the FLNA. The FLNA—the Front for the Liberation of North America—used the youth gangs from America's city streets as their armed force, led by professional terrorists, Communist agitators, and wanted men who infiltrated into the United States using assumed identities. The FLNA's announced purpose was the destruction of American society, the overthrow of the United States Government, the establishment of a "people's government," although which people the FLNA had in mind seemed obvious—themselves.

It was a second American Revolution, but it bore little resemblance to the original. Rather than fighting for liberty, the FLNA fought with terror against the very foundations of liberty.

The FLNA's revolution started with transformer topplings, derailments, then spread to violence in the streets, assassinations and robberies, arsenal thefts, portions of cities burned out and abandoned, commercial aircraft sabotaged, and the firebombings of churches and synagogues. Few were stupid enough or bold enough to go out after dark, and curfews were in effect everywhere, as were other restrictions on the previously taken-for-granted American way.

Among the first casualties were individual liberties. First among these assaulted by a well-intentioned but drastically ill-prepared government was the right to keep and bear arms. With the de facto temporary suspension of the Second Amendment, the persisting violence, fueled by the prohibition of legal firearms and ammunition sales, grew, and other traditional constitutional liberties had to be curtailed as well: freedom of assembly, because those who assembled had to be observed, as they might be FLNA or provoke the violence of the FLNA's wrath; freedom of speech, because those who preached against the FLNA might be Patriot sympathizers and had to be observed in the hope that they might eventually aid in uncovering a Patriot cell; freedom of the press, because so much information was classified and such previously innocent items as notices of public meetings, announcements of public appearances by celebrities or dignitaries, schedules of any kind—all of these could be used by the FLNA. Travel restrictions. Searches without warrants.

As the restrictions grew, so did the body count. The death toll was already staggering and was mounting almost exponentially.

And now the electoral process itself was under attack. Across the nation, local, state, and some federal offices were at stake, but to the FLNA all that was at stake was power. If elections could be disrupted or manipulated, all the better.

Such was the reason, Holden reflected, that before five in the morning he, a Ph.D. and former history professor, and Rosie Shepherd, a former detective with Metro PD, were running along the perimeter of a deflection barrier set up beyond the main fence of the private estate of Roger Costigan.

Costigan, millionaire business executive, law-and-order candidate in the Metro mayoral elections, was controlled by the FLNA. The more violence the FLNA wrought, the more assured of victory Costigan would be, the more assured of defeat Costigan's liberal opponent, Harris Gamby.

David Holden skidded to the ground on his knees, catching his breath as lights suddenly came on in the south garden. Rosie Shepherd dropped to her knees beside him. "This was a bum idea, David."

The third member of their party dropped to hands and knees, breathing hard, muttering something unintelligible.

Holden looked at Rosie and smiled, although he knew she couldn't see his smile. "You're right—but it was the only idea we had. Okay?"

He heard the soft sound of her gentle laughter and she whispered back, "Okay."

"Not okay, all right? We're gonna get fuckin' killed. Those guys got guns."

David Holden looked at Anthony Scapalini. "When you were a full-time safecracker, what kind of places did you rob? Homes for the aged?"

"Funny. Very fuckin' funny." Scapalini was still breathing hard.

Before the coming of the FLNA, David Holden's life had been peaceful, predictable. He'd liked it that way. His modest salary as a university professor was augmented by his illustrations for science-fiction short stories and the occasional cover assignment for a science-fiction novel. Before the coming of the FLNA the most excitement he had had was an occasional outing in the deer woods. Or a symposium at some other university (a good excuse at times for a cheap family vacation). Or an invitation to a science-fiction convention, where he would meet with people of divergent backgrounds united by a common interest. Despite his SEAL team days, the peace and calm were welcome.

His greatest worries had been paying his bills on time. Or getting through his Naval Reserve duty, so bland by comparison to his earlier Navy days.

Because the Patriots fought back and refused to be disarmed, they did what the law could not and hit the FLNA hard rather than standing by and witnessing the destruction of the United States. The Patriots were wanted men and women, considered by some to be greater enemies of democracy than the FLNA, blamed by liberal-biased media as the cause of the violence, labeled as being reactionary armed lunatics, more sought out for retribution by officialdom than the child killers and church bombers themselves.

Luther Steel had told David Holden that Holden—his face on the cover of newsmagazines, Sunday supplements, and on posters in post offices everywhere—was the most wanted man in America.

Defending his country and avenging the FLNA murder of his wife and three children had brought him this distinction.

And now he was about to become a burglar.

CHAPTER 3

Luther Steel sat up in bed, his apartment totally dark.

He had awakened at precisely 4:00 A.M., gotten out of bed and urinated, then gone back to bed. Sleep was impossible. He thought, reset the clock so the alarm going off at four could never be checked. Don't turn on the lights so no one wonders why you were awake when the Costigan estate was entered. Cover your act.

He sat in the darkness, was one with it. He wondered absently if he were white would his hands have stood out more in the darkness or less because the sheet that covered him below the waist was white? He dismissed the thought.

At precisely 5:00 A.M., David Holden and Rose Shepherd would enter the grounds of the Roger Costigan estate. There would be a power blackout, the transformer serving the estate rigged to go out by Holden, Holden using his SEAL team training again. When the Costigan estate's reserve generator kicked on automatically, it would immediately kick off. That was thanks to Clark Pietrowski, who had arranged that the gasoline supply already within the generator and the reserve supply were both sugared, through the help of the swimming-pool maintenance crew. Pietrowski had helped Metro PD bust the owner of the maintenance company ten years ago, then gone to bat helping the man get his bank loan to start the pool maintenance company after his parole. The generator would sputter on for a few minutes, then die. The Costigan estate would be in total darkness and its alarm

15

system would be silenced. He'd run the plan for a break-in past Director Cerillia, the plan's purpose to garner some leads that could be pursued to help get Costigan. Rudolph Cerillia had remarked, "These are extraordinary times, Luther. I can't officially authorize a break-in, but it seems like the only way if this Costigan is being backed by the FLNA. We can't let him walk in as mayor of Metro on a law-and-order ticket, can we? And if there's no other means by which we can even get an investigation started, well—go for it."

On the nightstand beside Steel was his Sig-Sauer P-226 9mm. Between the mattress and boxspring was the little Smith & Wesson Model 66 2½. America was now a place where one gun might not be quite enough, not only on the street but in the home.

Steel thought of his wife and children. It was Central time where they lived, under assumed names, protected, but they would have been asleep anyway. Although he missed his family, he was grateful they were not in Metro. Metro had become the most violent city in the United States since the coming of the FLNA and the restrictions on civil liberties forced on all levels of law enforcement by a blindly reacting and terrified Congress. And as agent-in-charge of the Federal Bureau of Investigation's Special Task Force in Metro, it seemed reasonable to assume that the Front for the Liberation of North America wanted him dead and wouldn't have minded killing his family, and would probably have delighted in their deaths.

He wondered if David Holden and Rosie Shepherd had made it inside yet. He looked at the clock. No—but it was nearly time for the penetration.

Costigan had a safe, but would Costigan be stupid enough to keep incriminating documents there?

Pietrowski had taken care of the safe as well, by means of one Anthony Scapalini, "the safecracker's safecracker," as Pietrowski had put it. But a real flake.

Luther Steel wished he smoked. At least he could have gotten out of bed and done something.

CHAPTER 4

The deflection barrier ended where the ditch began. Running along the edge of the ditch—it was wider than a normal man could safely count on jumping and the base of the ditch was packed with broken glass— brought them to the pecan grove. Through the pecan grove the footing in pitch darkness was uncertain because of the nuts, which made for a surface like crackly marbles. Beyond the pecan grove there was the lake, the water level down because the summer had been hot and dry, a defoliated collar surrounding the water. They ran along the edge of the lake and up to the electrified fence; barbed wire, which was also electrified, topped it. This was the only location where the fence could be easily accessed and, because of that, there was added security—photoelectric eyes, hypersensitive microphones, and video surveillance cameras—in place.

All of the security operated electrically.

David Holden checked the Rolex on his left wrist. The time was exactly 4:59 P.M., all watches for the operation synchronized. He watched the movement of his watch's sweep second hand, Rosie, beside him, peering over his shoulder, her breath against his face. Behind them Holden could hear Anthony Scapalini breathing hard and cursing softly.

Five A.M.

The lights—security lights, porch lights, patio lights, all the lights—went out. The long, landscaped lawn on the other side of the fence and the swimming pool beyond suddenly vanished in darkness.

"Let's go," Holden hissed. He jumped to his feet, running toward the fence, ticking off seconds, the security lights flickering on, then off. So much for the emergency generator.

Holden and Rosie reached the fence. Holden didn't look back for Scapalini the safecracker, figuring he'd be along. Rosie reached for the fence. Holden held her back, drawing his left hand from the pocket of his BDU pants, with a plastic bag full of metal shavings he'd garnered with a hacksaw and a piece of steel pipe. He opened the plastic bag, tossing it open-end-forward toward the fence. Not a single spark.

Holden touched the fence, gingerly moved his hands up and down along it and then right and left.

"Now?"

He looked at Rosie and smiled, answering her by taking three long steps back, then hurtling himself against the fence, already into the climb. The fence rattled noisily under his weight, despite the rapidity with which he moved. The guards he'd seen earlier, if they were anywhere in earshot, would hear him. But that was a calculated risk. The chain link was tough to navigate with the relatively inflexible toe design of his combat boots, but he reached the top nonetheless, his gloved left hand grabbing for the barbed wire, tugging a strand toward him. Rosie was below him as he looked down, the rectangle of vinyl skinned from the front seat of an abandoned car sailing up toward him. He caught it neatly, snaked it over the barbed wire, then rolled over the fence. He grabbed onto the chain link on the other side, swinging there for a moment, getting a foothold, then jumping clear. Holden came down on all fours in a deep crouch, his right hand moving to the butt of the H&K submachine gun slung tight at his right side. His left hand loosened the sling, and Holden stabbed the submachine gun forward against the darkness, looking right and left, dodging into the deeper shadows a few feet from the fence beside a small wooden toolshed. The toolshed was built as an exact miniature replica of the sprawling, turn-of-the-century-style country house beyond.

Rosie Shepherd was helping Scapalini over the fence. Scapalini looked to be miserably out of shape, confirming Holden's earlier assumptions about the man.

Scapalini was at the top of the fence now, awkwardly clambering over it where the vinyl shielded him against the barbed wire. Holden heard the distant sound of a voice, then another—closer—responding, the words indistinguishable. The guards, of course.

As Scapalini started down Holden safed the MP5 SD3 and ran for the fence, half catching Scapalini, Holden reasoning that a safecracker with a broken ankle or leg was no safecracker at all. He broke Scapalini's fall instead, half dragging the man back into the shadows. Rosie nimbly flipped the top of the fence, came down along the chain link for a few feet, then jumped clear. She landed on her feet, like a cat, coming up out of the crouch with her 9-mm submachine gun—identical to his own—in both hands. It had seemed like a crime not to avail themselves of some of the weapons and equipment in place in the subterranean base to which Steel had introduced them. And Luther Steel had agreed that they should. There seemed, indeed, to be some advantages in the left-handed clandestine affiliation with the President of the United States, Director Cerillia, and Steel's FBI Special Task Force. But David Holden, at the back of his mind, pondered what hidden disadvantages might come to haunt him.

Rosie moved into the shadows beside Holden.

Scapalini was muttering something. Holden ignored him. He told Rosie, whispering, "Like we planned it, you 'shepherd' our little pal here."

" 'Shepherd'—very funny." Rosie Shepherd nodded.

Holden peered around the corner of the building. The guards whose voices he had heard earlier were gone now. The fence had rattled loudly enough as Holden, Rosie, and Scapalini the safecracker crossed it, and the guards might have heard it. There was nothing to do about it if they had.

David Holden moved from the modest cover and concealment the shed provided and into the manicured greensward, shadows darker than the night everywhere beneath the towering poplars and Georgia pines. The grass felt wet with dew and smelled clean, almost freshly cut. He kept moving, glancing back once. Rosie and Scapalini were following him.

He cut the distance to the pool area by half, crouching beside a neatly trimmed, rectangularly shaped hedgerow, listening. Distant voices could be heard. He could make out nothing of what was said. In the house beyond the pool there were flickering, fleeting shafts of light—flashlights, he imagined. They were visible through the broad, evenly spaced windows, which, even if he hadn't memorized the house's floor plan, would have clearly delineated the boundaries between one room and the next.

Again, Rosie was beside him.

Holden didn't risk speaking, instead signaled to her with his hands that he had heard several voices from well beyond the pool area. She nodded.

Holden moved ahead, toward the pool area. There was open greensward here, like the fairway on a golf course with no cover. He ran. Beyond the pool just ahead were white double glass doors with very small panes of glass. It was through these doors that he intended to go.

He neared the pool, the smell of chlorine nauseatingly strong, a voice nearby now, then another. Holden threw himself down behind a free-standing white-painted wooden cupboard. The smell of chlorine was stronger here where the pool chemicals were kept.

The voices drew nearer: ". . . fuckin' generator went like that."

"We're bein' hit, damnit. This ain't no fuckin' coincidence. Shit . . ."

Holden peered around the corner of the cupboard. The two men who belonged to the voices were clearly visible. If they kept walking in the same direction, they'd bump into Rosie and Scapalini.

Holden let both men move past.

To kill them would have been easy, but there was no moral justification. They worked for Costigan, but might well be just hired security. They sounded a little on the foul-mouthed side, but that wasn't reason enough to kill them. Besides, these days that would have qualified half the population for the death penalty.

He unslung the H&K submachine gun, making certain that where he set it was dry, rose into a crouch, and moved from behind the cupboard. As the Defender knife come into his right fist, the scraping sound of steel against leather was maddeningly loud to him but, realistically, something neither man probably heard.

The Defender in his right fist like a dagger, he moved toward the nearer of the two men, also the larger. The man started to turn around, but Holden's body was already into a jumping forward kick, the left leg snapping up and out, snapping down for added momentum as his right leg stomped forward, both feet off the ground for an instant, the flat of his right foot impacting the larger of the security men squarely between the shoulder blades, felling him like an ax through a tree, his body skidding across the concrete apron surrounding the pool.

As the second man wheeled toward him, a gun

rising in his right hand, Holden wheeled into a round-house kick, Holden's left foot striking the inside of the second man's forearm, the gun almost popping from his fingers, arcing up, dropping like a rock into the pool. Holden stepped inside what remained of the man's guard, the heel of Holden's left hand impacting the base of the second man's chin, his right knee smashing up into the stomach. The head snapped back, then forward, the body jackknifing. Holden raked the butt of the Crain Defender down along the left side of the man's head, putting him out.

Holden felt the first man moving before he saw it. A normal man would have been down for the count after the full impact kick Holden had delivered, but the first of the two security men was apparently made of tougher stuff. Holden sidestepped left, almost losing his balance and going into the pool as the man rushed past him, then fell to his knees, Holden starting for him. But there was a pistol in the man's right hand, too slender in the slide for a .45, maybe a Browning High Power. Holden didn't have time to ponder the question.

Holden started for one of the Berettas.

There was a flash of movement.

Rosie Shepherd, her left leg fully extended, right leg folded under, her body bent slightly at the waist, hit the man on the right shoulder with her left foot. The pistol fell from his fingers, skittered across the cement, his body rocking forward. As he fell Holden was on him, the knife still in his right fist as his fist crossed the man's jaw. The head snapped back as the body went limp.

Holden felt for a pulse as Rosie dropped to her knees beside him. "He's alive."

"Tough bastard," Rosie observed.

Holden just looked at her for an instant. Then he was up, checking the second man. Like the first, he was only unconscious and seemed to be breathing regularly. Using plastic restraints, they bound the men at wrists and ankles. Gagging an unconscious person could lead to respiratory distress and subsequent death, so they left them bound only.

Scapalini stood by while Holden and Rosie dragged the two unconscious men behind the chemical cupboard. She caught up the first man's gun—it was a Browning High Power—dumped the magazine and the chambered round into the pool, and tossed the gun into the bushes.

Holden checked his watch. They were already behind schedule. By 5:23 the power would be restored and the sugared gasoline in the emergency generator wouldn't matter anymore. It was 5:12.

They reached the double doors beyond the pool, Scapalini still lagging behind. With no operational alarm system, it didn't matter how the doors were opened, so Holden took the Defender knife and pried it between the doors, then brought it down hard, spine first. There was a latch bolt only (by the feel of it) and not a block-style dead bolt. As a young boy Holden had seen the Australian actor Scott Forbes, as Jim Bowie, do the same thing in the television series based on the heroic frontiersman and his equally heroic blade, and he had wanted to try it ever since. It worked. The knife in his right hand, his left hand turning one of the door handles, the theme from the old TV show suddenly running through his head—the Ken Darby Singers singing a cappella—David Holden stepped through.

There was a sitting room beyond the doors and, even in darkness, the furnishings looked impressive.

Rosie Shepherd came through behind him, Scapalini in tow, his backpack still in his hands like a laundry sack.

The safe was in Costigan's office and Costigan's office was at the far end of the house.

They kept moving, up a single step rising from the sitting room into a broad open hallway, the hallway like a low divider between the sitting room and a high-ceilinged room beyond. However traditional the house appeared from the outside, it was modern and spacious within. He followed the hallway until it stopped at double wooden doors. He thought he might need to do the trick with the knife again, but the doors—almost disappointingly—opened easily. Rosie stepped through beside him, her submachine gun in a hard assault position beside her right hip. The doors separated the main portion of the house from what amounted to Costigan's office wing, a holding room for visitors, an outer office for a secretary and his inner office suite.

They moved into the holding room quickly, no windows here and a flashlight necessary for the first time. Holden drew the little Mini-Mag Lite, twisted it on, swept the holding room, then narrowed the beam to a single shaft of white light. Beside him, Rosie Shepherd did the same. When Holden glanced behind them he saw Scapalini following.

Into the outer office. Holden almost tripped on a lamp cord, stumbled against a table. Rosie hissed under her breath, "Clumsy."

"Hmm," Holden whispered back. The door to Costigan's inner office suite was locked.

Holden turned to Scapalini. "How quickly," Holden whispered, "can you get us through this door?"

"Not quick enough to get into the safe."

Holden shrugged, looked at Rosie.

They shifted their submachine guns behind them, stepped back, stepped toward the door and kicked simultaneously. The door vibrated, then fell partially inward, hanging on one hinge. Rosie kicked at it again and the door collapsed. In a normal conversational tone she said, "Well, if they didn't know we were here . . ." She let the rest of the sentence hang.

Holden pushed Scapalini through the door, hanging back, his eyes shifting toward the open double doors on the far side of the holding room. It was 5:16, leaving seven minutes to hit the safe. Once the power came on, if they were still inside the room and the safe had been tampered with, steel shutters would automatically activate, and steel door panels as well, trapping them inside.

"Hurry him up," Holden rasped, back-stepping through the room, waiting for the inevitable now.

The inner office suite was larger than most apartments, the desk oddly small in comparison; several couches, overstuffed leather chairs, and a long bar dominated the room.

Rosie was taking what looked like an original Jackson Pollock painting down from the wall, Scapalini less than enthusiastically helping her. Set into the wall behind, where the painting had been, was the vault door.

"Ain't enough time," Scapalini groused.

Rosie Shepherd put the muzzle of the submachine gun beside his right cheek. "Better hope there is, my dishonest little friend."

Scapalini opened his pack.

David Holden had seen his share of big heist films over the years, but that was where his knowledge of safecracking ended. There was something that looked like a very chunky calculator that Scapalini attached magnetically to the door beside the combination dial. Tubes ran out from it like tubes from a physician's stethoscope, and Scapalini positioned the earpieces as his fingers played over the buttons on the calculatorlike device like the hands of a pianist over a keyboard. His right hand moved to the combination dial, and whatever impressions of awkwardness or slowness David Holden had formed of the prima donna-ish Scapalini vanished. It was evident that here was a man with true mastery of an art.

"You don't need to hold the light on the dial for me, but it doesn't bother me if you want to."

"What are you doing?" Rosie Shepherd asked abruptly.

"I could try a mathematical progression of likely combinations and if I hit even one coordinate, the sensing device would blink and give me the number. But that would take too long. So I'm using the sensing device along with listening for the combination, feeling the tension in my fingers—you got twenty years, I can teach you how to do it maybe half as good as me. So shut up and let me work, huh, Detective?"

Rosie Shepherd merely nodded. Holden remembered to take his eyes from the safe door long enough to go and check the doors from the holding room to the hallway. Nothing so far.

As he returned to the oversized wall safe, Scapalini murmured, "Got it."

"The safe?" Holden said, feeling stupid for saying it.

"No—my Aunt Tillie's dentures—yeah, but only one digit. But it's workin'. Some boxes don't crack like this." And Scapalini went back to work.

Holden gave a nod to Rosie, Rosie taking off in a long-strided run for the inner-office-suite door, then disappearing into the outer office. Holden set the selector of the MP5 / SD3 to full auto. It was 5:20, exactly. Three minutes to get the safe open and get out of the room. Holden went to the desk. The drawers weren't locked so he didn't bother looking inside. He felt beneath it, found no evidence of secret compartments. There was a switch—apparently an emergency call button. It looked as though it would have to be activated by the foot, just inside the skirt at the front. His memory of Costigan from newspaper and magazine photos was of a tall man long-legged enough to reach the button without looking like he was doing it. Nothing would be kept in the secretary's files, he reasoned, at least nothing incriminating.

Just trying the office safe was a long shot. Costigan would have had to be foolhardy or overconfident to—

"I got it!" Holden ran toward the safe, looking at his watch. Two minutes and a few seconds remained. Scapalini threw open the safe door, stepping aside as he did. "Knew a guy who got his brains shot out when he opened a safe. A shotgun trap."

"Right." Holden nodded. "Get your stuff and join Rosie in the holding room. Watch out she knows it's you."

"So—you mean we can leave?"

"Yeah—just a few seconds." Holden turned his attention to the contents of the safe, the little flashlight's beam on its widest dispersal. A record book. He opened it. Accounts. He dropped it in the little musette bag at his left side. An envelope. Inside the envelope was a stack of bills, twenties, fifties, and hundreds. He left them. If he had known what he was looking for . . . "Shit . . ." A book inside a transparent plastic sleeve. It was leather-bound. The binding almost crumbled when he moved it. On impulse he put the book as gently as he could into the musette bag. Some jewelry. A handgun—just as Chief's Special, the blued variety with a three-inch heavy barrel and a square butt.

Again on impulse he took the envelope of cash, feeling dirty inside, like a thief.

Holden looked at his watch. Fewer than thirty seconds remained. He left the safe door open, glanced across the floor to be sure that Scapalini hadn't left any of his tools. He broke into a run for the inner-office-suite door.

Holden's eyes squinted involuntarily against the

blinding light. So much for wristwatch synchronization, he thought fleetingly. He hurtled himself toward the door. From above the door behind the paneling set there, a steel door was dropping, steel shutters closing—snap, snap, snap—over the windows. Holden heard Rosie shouting, "David!" Holden jumped, hit the floor halfway through the doorway, and rolled, the door crashing downward and slamming shut behind him.

He looked up into Rosie's pretty face. "Hi!"

CHAPTER 5

Luther Steel tried to sound sleepy when he answered the telephone, letting it ring three times—all the suspense he could take—before answering it. "This is Steel."

"Just listen, Luther." It was Clark Pietrowski's voice. "The you-know-what came on early. They may be in deep shit." The phone clicked off dead. It was evident that Pietrowski didn't trust the phone as safe for communication and that was wise. The power. It came on early. What if Holden and Detective Shepherd and Pietrowski's crazy safecracker friend were trapped inside?

Luther Steel stood up, naked. He walked across the bedroom to where his weights were. He picked up the two thirty-pound dumbbells, began curling them in unison. He needed forties, hadn't been able to afford them and couldn't justify putting them on his expense account. The taxpayers shouldn't pay for his fitness training.

If the phone rang again, would it be Pietrowski telling him everything was all right? Or everything was gone bad? He licked his lips.

He could feel the sweat starting to slick his skin. He kept working the dumbbells, got to thirty repetitions, and put them down. Next, the chest puller. He picked it up, raised it over his head, and flexed, expanding it straight outward on both sides.

If Costigan's people nailed Holden, Shepherd, and Scapalini, Costigan would be a shoo-in for the mayoral election, and his FLNA backers would essentially rule the city. And if, somehow, it was learned that the FBI—even unofficially—was behind the break in . . . Luther Steel set down the chest puller, picked up his dumbbells, and started knocking out another double set. "Damn . . ."

CHAPTER 6

They ran along the greensward now, Holden and Rosie propelling Scapalini between them. Lights were coming on all over the estate, the pool lights flickering to life as Holden looked back. At least three men were after them, all three with long guns, indistinguishable at that distance. Alarms were sounding everywhere.

Toward the fence.

They reached the fence but could not cross it because of the high voltage. Holden's mind raced. They had planned for such an unlikely contingency. "Hang a left," Holden called out, Rosie turning, Holden pushing Scapalini along.

"I'm gonna have a heart attack!"

"You're gonna be dead if we try going over that fence," Holden told him, running. Gunfire came from behind them. Assault rifles. Holden stabbed the MP5 SD3 behind him, firing at an upward angle so he wouldn't kill. He let out a long burst, then another and another. "Why the hell—"

"They're only security guards, all right?" Holden called to Rosie. "Get to the garage—I got Scapalini."

Rosie sprinted ahead.

About two hundred yards from their present position, on the far side of the poplars and Georgia pines, was located the estate's personal-car garage (to be distinguished from the estate maintenance vehicles). Costigan had six cars, two Cadillacs, a Ford station wagon, a Mercedes—Holden couldn't remember which model—and two Porsches, both 944s. Rosie had one set of Porsche master keys provided by a Patriot who was also an automobile dealer.

More gunfire. Holden didn't waste an answering burst. "Hurry, man!" Holden shouted to Scapalini.

Once through the line of trees, Scapalini tripped, dropping his bag. Holden caught up the bag, dragging Scapalini to his feet and pushing him on.

The garage was a miniature version of the house. From inside there was the roar of an engine coming to life. In the distance Holden heard police sirens.

The two Porsches were parked side by side, one red, one white. Rosie was in the white one. "Slide over!" Holden shouted, letting Scapalini fall to his knees at the edge of the concrete apron that opened onto the two-lane-wide black-topped driveway. The second Porsche was the only vehicle of the remaining five that had a realistic chance of catching them, although the Mercedes might have a slim chance if a good driver were at the wheel. To be on the safe side, Holden aimed the H&K submachine gun toward the red Porsche, blowing out the front tires, then aimed it at the Mercedes, doing the same.

The magazine was empty. There was no time to reload. Holden shoved his submachine gun through the open doorway and jumped behind the wheel. "You ever drive one of these?" Rosie Shepherd asked him.

"No. You?"

"No."

"Good—then I won't look so dumb." He threw it into first, almost forgot the emergency brake, stomped the gas and let up on the clutch, and the car lurched ahead with more power than he'd ever experienced in first gear with any car.

He skidded to a stop near Scapalini, who was running for the car. Rosie was out, launching him into the backseat, then falling inside, slamming the door as Holden hit the gas. The rear end fishtailed, Holden fighting the wheel, wanting to downshift, nothing to downshift to, upshifting and stomping the gas again, the Porsche seeming to fly under him. He was on the blacktop, shifted to third more smoothly, getting the feel of the car.

Gunfire came from the left, bullets pinging off the bodywork, the windshield spiderwebbing. "Those guys know what one of these cost?" It was Scapalini, sounding breathless from his run.

"I guess they don't," was all Holden could answer.

Ahead of them, pulling across the two-lane driveway, was a full-sized pickup truck, two armed men jumping out, taking cover behind it, opening fire.

"I gotta try an' nail those bastards!" Rosie Shepherd shouted.

"I know!" Holden called back to her, shifting into fourth for a minute, double-clutching as he downshifted into third, the Porsche eating up the road.

Bullets skated across the hood.

Rosie Shepherd's submachine gun opened fire, the passenger-side window in the pickup truck shattering, the left rear tire blowing.

More gunfire sprayed toward them.

Holden's left hand grasped the butt of the smaller of the two Berettas. He wrenched it from beneath his left armpit, thumbing the safety up and off, stabbing the 92F Compact through the driver's-side window and firing, his right fist locked to the steering wheel.

The mirror shattered beside his left hand and he almost dropped the pistol but was unhurt. He kept firing. A burst of submachine-gun fire from Rosie Shepherd beside him. Scapalini shouted, "We're all gonna be killed!"

"You bet!" Holden agreed loudly, dropping the emptied Beretta between his legs, his left hand on the wheel, his right on the stick, downshifting into second as he cut the wheel hard right, then left, off the road surface and into the shrubbery, the Porsche's rear end stalling for an instant. Holden looked back as he downshifted, then stomped the gas, a wake of dirt and plant debris showering up on both sides of the Porsche as it lurched ahead. Holden shifted to second, gunfire blasted from the pickup truck as Rosie Shepherd shouted to him, "Don't lean forward!" She fired past him with the submachine gun. He could feel the passage of the bullets through the air—or at least he thought he could.

He told Rosie, "Stop that," then cut the wheel left as he downshifted, the engine roaring, the tachometer almost redlining. They were back on the asphalt. He stomped the clutch and revved, changing from first to third, skipping second, playing the clutch—it wasn't his car anyway—to retard the engine a little as he built RPMs, then letting the clutch all the way up, the Porsche coughing once and firing ahead. He kept it in third.

The front gates. They weren't supposed to be electrified. But they were wrought iron. He thought better of that, downshifting into second, cutting the wheel right, back onto the grass, the rear end fishtailing maddeningly. He downshifted into first, the front end bearing right no matter how he steered. He upshifted, the Porsche lurching forward. The chain link fence was ahead. It was electrified. The car was grounded. He hoped for the best.

"Don't touch anything metal!"

"What?"

"Shut up, Scapalini—would ya just shut up?" The tachometer almost redlining again as he bounced into the greensward on the opposite side of the house, cutting the wheel left, shifting, stomping the gas.

"David!"

Holden looked at Rosie Shepherd, shrugged his shoulders. She formed the words "I love you" with her lips. He nodded, shifted into third, riding the clutch, then double-clutched and downshifted as they hit the fence.

Chunks of chain link formed a storm of metal around them, within the storm bolts of electricity arcing across the hood, Holden seeing it in slow motion even though it took less than a second. He shifted, powered through, downshifted, and rode the brakes hard as he turned onto the road outside.

"Holy shit!" Scapalini exclaimed.

David Holden said nothing.

Rosie Shepherd was saying a Hail Mary.

CHAPTER 7

Dimitri Borsoi heard the telephone ringing at the edge of his dream. He opened his eyes. The room around him was gray with early light. The dream was gone. The ringing of the telephone remained.

He reached across, fumbled the receiver, almost knocking his Glock pistol off the end of the nightstand, brought the receiver to his ear. "Yes?"

"Johnson—look—we've got very deep trouble."

"Costigan—why are you calling me?" He looked at his Timex. "Why are you calling me at six-fifteen?"

"There's been a break-in."

Borsoi sat up, found his cigarettes, lit one. "At your house?"

"I know I shouldn't have—"

"Your safe?"

"Yes, but—"

"You are an asshole of the first rank, Costigan. You didn't have—"

"A book—"

"One of your special books, right?"

"It was locked in the safe. It must be the government. The electric power got shut off. I figured it was your people doing it, toppled another transformer or something. But the emergency generator was tampered with. One of my men here thinks someone put sugar into the gasoline used for it. The book I mentioned, my account book, that envelope of money—"

"Hang up your telephone now. I will contact you. Report the break-in, not the specifics of it. I will contact you. Blame the FLNA for the break-in. That is

37

all that you can do. Hang up now." Borsoi hung up, not caring what Costigan did for the moment. The government was getting smart.

He looked at the woman beside him, making certain she was still asleep, watching her intently. If she'd overheard, he would have to kill her. . . .

Luther Steel's telephone rang out and he didn't wait for three rings or try faking sleepiness in his voice. "Yes!"

"They made it." It was Pietrowski and the line clicked dead.

Steel hung up the phone. He looked at his watch. It was almost time to be up and rolling away, and at least his workout was taken care of.

He walked into the kitchen, filled the tea kettle. He wished his wife and children were here, but was glad that they weren't. . . .

They were in the studio's living-room area, Holden sitting on the couch, Rosie kneeling beside him, the book on the coffee table. Clark Pietrowski was smoking a cigarette, staring at the book. "When will Luther be here?" Rosie Shepherd asked.

"Not until after nine. He can't make this place look obvious, Rosie."

Rosie Shepherd nodded.

Clark Pietrowski asked, "I give—what's this book?"

David Holden very gently turned the pages. "This is about a hundred and fifty years old. It's a sex manual. Underground sex manual."

"A what?" Pietrowski asked.

"A sex manual. Pretty racy stuff. It's in Latin. Probably a 'modern' printing of something from the Renaissance period. I'd have to be a lot more familiar with Latin that I am to tell. But it's a sex manual."

"Is it valuable?" Rosie asked him.

"I would think so. Like I said, my Latin's nothing to jump up and down about, but from what I can make out, it looks like reasonably graphic stuff."

"Pornography?" Rosie said, sounding incredulous. "Roger Costigan collects pornography?"

"Yeah, well—it's the special kind, that's what would make this so unique." Holden exhaled, reaching to the table, mooching one of Rosie's cigarettes and her lighter to fire it with.

"How special is it?" Pietrowski grinned. "That kind of—"

Rosie Shepherd snapped, "Cut it out, huh? I'm a big person. What are we talking about?"

David Holden looked at her, shrugged, felt embarrassed saying it. "Well, it's, ah—seems to be all about, ah—about older men having intimate sexual relations with . . ."

"Young . . ." Rosie Shepherd's hands went to her mouth, Holden smiling as she started to flush. Rough, tough Metro detective and juvenile officer and now freedom fighter . . . was blushing.

"Young boys?" Pietrowski said.

"Yeah. Roger Costigan's interests may be considerably more diversified than we imagined," David Holden said, exhaling smoke and watching it rise toward the black-painted ceiling.

CHAPTER 8

Luther Steel stepped out of his car in front of the Coke machine. It really was an antique. He checked his bumper. It barely touched the machine but the car wasn't full-size anyway so there'd be enough room.

Steel looked for the right change and started feeding money to the machine. Steel pushed the selection buttons. He felt the now customary lurch and the platform beneath his feet started to descend. His eyes stayed on the Coke machine and he smiled as he realized that all this time he had been feeding money to the machine, he'd never gotten a Coke from it.

The platform continued descending.

He closed his eyes against the contrasting brightness of day and the darkness at the level of the platform and the suddenly very bright light coming from the cavernous opening below. He had never been specifically told what the base was constructed for but assumed it was a Delta flight base that for some reason had been abandoned.

There was a pneumatic thumping sound, the slapping of gaskets, and the light from below shifted to red, Steel squinting his eyes against it and then opening them fully.

The platform was still moving downward. Steel looked, and one of the electric carts was visible about twenty-five feet below him. Pietrowski had been thoughtful. Steel stuffed his hands into his pockets, rocked on his heels. He felt ten years younger than he had when the thing was still in the planning stage, ten years younger now that Holden and Detective Shepherd had penetrated Costigan's estate and successfully escaped.

As the platform stopped Steel approached the control panel. The hole in the ground above him couldn't just be left there for all the world to see. . . .

Rosie Shepherd watched Luther Steel as he went to the kitchen set, opened the refrigerator, and took out a can of Coke. "That elevator ride does it to me every time." Steel grinned, closing the refrigerator, the sound of the pop top resembling a pistol shot. It was so quiet here, she thought, so much like a television studio or something. If the underground facility really had been a Delta flight facility, why the television studio? That was the only thing that didn't make sense. The medical area, the kitchen area, the living-room area where they sat now, all of it like sets. Why?

She sat at David's feet, looking at the drawings in the book, line drawings, crudely executed, overly embellished and more crudely specific. Talk about not knowing how the other half lived, she thought. She turned the page. The next illustration looked anatomically impossible. "Ohh yuck—could somebody really do this?" she asked David and Clark Pietrowski, then felt herself smile as the two men looked at each other, looked uncomfortable, and neither of them answered. "I know—how would a couple of straight shooters like you guys know, right?"

Pietrowski lit another cigarette.

Luther Steel was standing over the table, looking down at the book. "This is what you got outta Costigan's place? He likes little boys?"

"Or at least books about them," David amended.

"And this record book," Pietrowski said, clearing his throat loudly. "Seems to be in some kind of code, Luther. Might be take money. Might be blackmail he's paying out. Either way, the envelope of money David found's gonna fit. Five G's—a lotta bucks to keep around the house, huh?"

Steel dug his hands into his pockets, rocked on his heels. "A rich guy like Costigan, maybe five thousand dollars isn't really that much. Who knows? Let's run a check on the money itself and see if there's anything dirty on it. Bill and Tom and Randy can run your leads for you. I want to take a long hard look at that book and figure out all the ins and outs."

She looked at David. "You mean this book?"

She'd never seen a black man blush before, but she guessed that was what he was doing now.

CHAPTER 9

She stood under the shower, letting the water stream across her body, just trying to make herself feel awake again. She'd had the same difficulty when she worked stake-out duty; with the sudden interruption of her normal sleep cycle, there was no way she could go to sleep again. Sleeping through the day always felt so sinful.

She turned the water to straight cold. Roger Costigan, Mr. Law and Order. She laughed at that, but it wasn't funny—sick maybe, but never funny. What he did with his personal life, of course, was his own business, but if it involved children that was another story. Working Juvenile, she'd seen child abuse and seen child abusers, and no matter what the reasons, what the excuses, what the justifications or rationalizations, the end result was always the same: Some child's life was ruined, now and forever.

There was always the possibility that Costigan only liked to read about the stuff or look at dirty pictures, always the possibility that the book was merely something he'd purchased for investment value and that was why it was stored in his safe. Somehow she hoped that was the reason for its being there. Somehow she doubted that it was.

Logic and years of experience dealing with crime of every description, some of it perpetrated by so-called upper-class people such as Roger Costigan, were at work in her and she couldn't resist the combined evidence. The cash, the record book, written in some kind of code, and the dirty book.

43

Roger Costigan was buying or selling. What? And what did payoffs and porno have to do with the Front for the Liberation of North America? She would have expected all of this from Harris Gamby, the liberal. Not a word from his mouth did she agree with; his ideas concerning the FLNA were not only juvenile, they were dangerous. In a period in which violence was rampant and the police were woefully overworked and tragically unable to protect the public, Gamby was calling for a Metro-wide ban on civilian handgun ownership of any kind and harsh restrictions on ownership and use of rifles and shotguns, all a prelude for national confiscatory gun legislation. He was calling for the disarming of off-duty police officers because so many had attempted to foil crimes in progress while off duty, resulting in injuries and some deaths. Gamby totally ignored the fact that being a cop was a twenty-four-hour-a-day job and even an unarmed cop would step in just because he or she was a cop. He was calling for jobs programs to turn youthful FLNA gangbangers away from the FLNA and into honest work. If the gangbangers had wanted jobs slinging hamburgers, they could have gotten them already, she thought. And he was calling for "peace talks" between the United States Government and the FLNA to mediate their differences and reach effective compromise. She wondered if Gamby would compromise with the devil? Gamby was tragically absurd. Roger Costigan uttered brave pronouncements concerning human rights, the Constitution, individual liberty, striking back at crime and criminals. But he was in the employ of the FLNA. Or was it all some trick? Was the man who implicated Costigan as an FLNA sympathizer assassinated by the fake nurse simply to make his story appear real? Was he merely an unwitting dupe?

She liked the showers here at the underground facility, whatever its original purpose. The sun showers they used in their camps were fine, but washing her hair took forever, rinsing it longer. And there was always a shortage of hot water, always someone standing in line to step in after her. Here she had all the water she wanted, all the time she needed to use it, could feel really clean.

At least before she thought about Costigan and the pornography.

Dimitri Borsoi sipped at his coffee, smoked his cigarette, and studied his problem. His problem's face stared up at him from the newspaper on the apartment's kitchen table: Roger Costigan, the people's choice for mayor of Metro. Metro was the key piece in the jigsaw puzzle he was carefully assembling, which, when completed, would bring the United States to its knees.

There were several possibilities of course. He could have Roger Costigan eliminated. Very easily, really. And then it would appear that Costigan had been martyred for his beliefs and some other law-and-order candidate could be found to step in at the last minute and face Harris Gamby, the newcomer winning handily against the idiot liberal Gamby. Maybe. How did American elections work? Gamby was losing in every poll, but could a newcomer be certified or whatever it took? Or would Gamby simply win by default?

Gamby would not make such a poor mayor for Metro, at least by FLNA standards. His social programs would be economically ruinous, his plan to totally disarm the citizenry would make FLNA operations substantially safer and the Patriots—damn them—substantially more obvious. But Gamby might change his opinions once he became acquainted with the realities of the job, and he couldn't be trusted to stay as politically naive and unintentionally cooperative as his campaign platform promised. If Gamby's ideas about peace talks between the United States and the FLNA caught the public imagination, it could prove immensely useful and help to accelerate the timetable for the toppling of the government. But everything that could be learned about Gamby suggested that, however stupid he might be, he was scrupulously honest and incorruptible.

There were other options, most obvious among them to tough it out with Costigan despite the book. Its origin in Costigan's safe could always be denied. After all, an interest in pornography—especially of that type—could be dismissed as trumped-up political slandering of the worst sort.

But what else had Costigan had in his wall safe?

If Roger Costigan had been so willing to tell about the dirty book, what was he hiding?

Dimitri Borsoi stubbed out his cigarette, hearing signs of the girl wakening. She had been very pleasant to be with the previous night, worshiped him as a revolutionary hero, might very well want to do it again. He was more than moderately interested in accommodating her. And there was plenty of time before other matters would be calling him away. . . .

Rose Shepherd volunteered—as the only woman of the company it was more or less expected of her, she realized—and cooked breakfast. She was never a fancy cook, but no one had ever complained that what she cooked was unpalatable. She was draining bacon on a paper-towel-covered plate, the men—David, Luther Steel, and old Clark Pietrowski—having moved their ruminations to the kitchen set, where she could cook for them without feeling excluded. She didn't know whether to consider it a compliment or condescension. There was no such thing as an apron in the underground facility, and she had a kitchen towel caught up around her waist protecting her blue jeans. She wiped her hands on it and returned to the fried eggs and cottage fried potatoes. David had offered to help and she had, of course, refused. Luther Steel was pouring himself coffee, asked if she wanted hers warmed up; she declined, not having touched the last cup.

David was speaking and she just liked to listen to the sound of his voice, a rich and unpretentious baritone that always sounded warm and firm. "What if the book—not the porno thing—but the other book, the accounts ledger or whatever it is—what if it's somehow tied in with the money we found in the safe?" She wanted a cigarette but her hands were too busy to bother with one. "Or what if it's something more than payoffs, but maybe a list of FLNA agents?" Interesting thought, but would Costigan be stupid or brazen enough or both to keep such a document in a personal safe?

"Costigan's got enough money and influence, he should have been able to insulate himself from anything illegal," Steel said. Stating the obvious, she thought. "My people have checked Costigan backwards and forwards and still nothing."

Clark Pietrowski took a dog-eared notebook out of an inside suit pocket, flipped through it while he fired another cigarette, then began to read. "Costigan is worth upwards of eighteen million dollars. His last tax return showed a gross income of $327,000 before adjustment. He was born into some money, not a lot, inherited a house that was in tax trouble and was loaded with antiques. He sold the antiques, used the money to pay off the taxes and refurbish the house and grounds, and sold the place for a hair under a half million. Those are 1970s dollars we're talking about. He used the money, or at least part of it, to buy up a few more houses, using the antiques inside to finance getting them out of tax hock and to fix 'em up. He found himself in the real estate business and the antique business. This was in suburban Chicago. In 1979 he moved to Metro, kept both businesses in Chicago, and got his antique business going down here too. All he's done with real estate in this state is to dabble, mostly personal stuff—"

Steel cut in. "Everything he's running down here is clean as a whistle."

"How about in Chicago?" Rose Shepherd asked over her shoulder.

"I don't know, Miss Shepherd—"

"Rose or Rosie—okay?"

"Rosie . . . If we start asking for background information on Roger Costigan, it's going to look pretty suspicious to a lot of people. It could blow this investigation wide open and destroy any chances we have for an arrest," Steel concluded.

She almost dropped the pan as she put David's sunny-side-up eggs—they looked disgusting—onto a plate for him. With all her years as a police officer, she had never once considered arresting Roger Costigan. How far had she come? So far that she knew she would never be able to go back.

She put bacon on David's plate. There were eleven pieces; she gave him four and ate one herself, leaving three each for Steel and Pietrowski. She started the other men's eggs. David was speaking again. "You going to Chicago, Luther?"

Before Steel could answer she put David's plate before him, saying, "Here, David. Just the way you like them."

David smiled at her.

"I'm planning on it," Steel answered David. "Clark here'll be in charge of the office, coordinate with you and Detective Shepherd for whatever you need. I'll be taking Bill Runningdeer with me. He used to work in Chicago and knows the city better than I do. I'm not letting the local Bureau office know we're coming. Someone might inadvertently leak it out to the wrong ears."

"Agreed," David said. "I think the only thing we can do is hit at the FLNA as hard as possible with the election coming up, maybe get them so involved fighting us they don't have as much time to budget for disrupting the election. And wait for what you find out in Chicago before taking any further action concerning Roger Costigan. I just wish we had more time. We're talking days now until the election."

She finished making eggs for Luther Steel and Clark Pietrowski: "Okay, guys, grab a plate and three pieces of bacon apiece," she announced.

"Don't you want anything?" David asked her.

She just lit a cigarette and sipped at her cold coffee.

CHAPTER 10

Dimitri Borsoi stepped into the car. It was time for a little revenge. Reefer was behind the wheel of the Chevrolet. "Is everyone ready, Reefer?"

"Yeah—everybody's all set, Mr. Johnson."

"That's good. Let's get going then." And Reefer glanced once over his shoulder and cut the wheel sharp to the left, the car lurched suddenly into traffic, and a screech of brakes from behind them brought a smile to Reefer's face. "Reefer, if we get into an accident, all that will serve to do is call attention to ourselves and cause some delay, neither of which is desirable, right?"

"You bet."

"Good—then try to drive like something a shade more intelligent than a drunken chimpanzee, hmm?"

Reefer glared at Borsoi for an instant. Borsoi glared back. Reefer looked ahead, both hands on the wheel. Borsoi shrugged his shoulders under his shoulder holster's harness. The Glock was a lightweight gun, but shoulder holsters never felt comfortable to him regardless of the make of the holster or the gun carried in it. A shoulder holster was the only practical thing, considering the heat and present circumstances. Police officers had begun routinely rousting anyone who wore his shirt outside of his trousers and might conceivably be carrying a gun. The heavy-fabric, loose-fitting shirt he wore (tucked in, or course) was the only answer. His left arm still hurt from when Detective Rose Shepherd had shot him in that truck-stop parking lot.

After several moments of silence and no more harrowing traffic experiences—Reefer was a satisfac-

tory driver when he wasn't trying to appear cool—
Reefer asked, "What's so special about this beaner
broad, Mr. Johnson?"

"Anna Comacho is the personal secretary for the
FBI's Special Task Force in Metro, Reefer. Getting to
her will be simpler than getting to Luther Steel or one
of his squad and just as effective, even more effective.
It'll anger them, of course, but more than that it will
show them they're vulnerable. And that's what we want
now."

Reefer nodded as if he understood, but Borsoi
doubted he did. As the gangbangers went, Reefer was
moderately intelligent, but his breadth and depth of
understanding of the world around him were sadly
lacking and interfered with his basic reasoning pro-
cesses, making all meaningful frame of reference non-
existent.

Reefer turned onto the expressway ramp with no
rapid acceleration, just easy and controlled. One thing
that was definitely in Reefer's favor was his adaptabil-
ity. He learned from mistakes, more than could be said
for his superior in the Leopards, the tall, lean, hard-
eyed Smitty. Smitty was so taken with himself that he
let others around him learn, never condescending to
do so himself. That made him doubly dangerous.
Reefer was never dangerous, only exasperating and
mildly annoying.

"So what's this broad like?" Reefer asked, apparently making idle conversation, blending the Chevrolet
into traffic.

"Anna Comacho? Well, she's a former secretary,
spent two years with Metro PD while she completed a
degree in accounting, then applied for a position with
the Federal Bureau of Investigation. She worked in
Washington for a few years, divorced her husband—
infidelity—and applied for a secretarial post in the

field. It's because of her police background, I imagine, that she was picked for Steel's Special Task Force."

"She carry a gun?"

"Not legally, but I imagine she does. She would be rather foolish not to. But it won't be with her. She has to pass through electronic security when she enters the Federal Office Building, and the only personnel allowed inside with weapons are those legally authorized. No exceptions." Borsoi looked at his wristwatch, checked their location on the expressway; they were right on time.

Reefer fell silent, apparently his ideas for intelligent conversation depleted. Borsoi took a nail clipper from his pocket and began trimming his fingernails. . . .

At ten o'clock every morning Anna Comacho left the Special Task Force offices and took the elevator to the main floor of the Federal Building. She would smile and wave at the security man, then exit the building and cross the broad expanse of the plaza surrounding it, jaywalk rather than go to the corner and go to the bakery across the street. She would spend anywhere from four to seven minutes inside the bakery and then exit the bakery with a box of sweet rolls and one chocolate doughnut, the doughnut for Clark Pietrowski. Borsoi reviewed these facts as he alternated his glance between the watch on his wrist and the doorway of the bakery.

Rain was starting to fall, heavily. It was needed, certainly, but not now. "Turn on the windshield wipers, Reefer."

What if Anna Comacho decided to wait out the storm?

What if the Leopard on the motorcycle couldn't handle his machine in the rain and missed his target?

And then Dimitri Borsoi saw her face, past shoulder-length hair in soft waves nearly as dark as the black skirt she wore. He spoke into his radio. "Be ready. When she reaches the curb on the Federal Building side, move." No reply was necessary. Anna Comacho's long-sleeved red blouse was already dotted by rain-drops. She looked silly in high heels and tight skirt with the white cardboard box clutched against her and a newspaper held over her head, running in short, inadequate steps. She was very pretty, which was a shame but would make what was about to happen doubly impactful.

Anna Comacho made it from the door to the curb and across the street in one almost perfect dash, hesitating a moment as a pickup truck nearly drove into her. She reached the opposite curb, running across the plaza toward the main entrance to the Federal Building.

Dimitri Borsoi looked to his left.

The motorcycle was jumping the curb onto the plaza directly opposite from her. The Leopard—in black leather, a dark-visored helmet over his head both hiding his face and protecting it from the contents of the container he carried—increased his speed.

Anna Comacho seemed to hesitate.

The Leopard was nearly on her.

With the window down, even over the roar of the motorcycle's engine, Borsoi could hear her screaming as the Leopard tossed the contents of the container into her face. She dropped to her knees, still screaming. The Leopard bounced over the near curb, into traffic, and around the corner. In seconds, pursuit would be impossible.

Dimitri Borsoi looked toward the plaza. No one was coming to help her. But eventually someone would. There was still an adequate albeit diminishing supply of well-intentioned fools. She was holding her face and screaming, then collapsed into the puddle into which she'd fallen.

"All right, Reefer. This time it worked very smoothly. Let's go."

Carefully this time, his face a little ashen, Reefer turned the car away from the curb and into traffic.

Borsoi looked back. Anna Comacho still lay in the puddle, all alone. . . .

The news of the horrible thing was on the radio. David Holden hugged Rosie Shepherd closer to him as they listened to Lem Parrish. Lem Parrish was a Patriot. There was static because they were driving farther out of the station's broadcast range by the mile. Parrish had stayed on the air and was co-anchoring the microphone for the late morning show with its regular host, a woman whose name Holden couldn't remember. "I think the murders discovered by the police this morning are ample proof that the last thing the FLNA wants anywhere in this country is a free election. I have a caller. Go ahead. You're on the air."

"Hello, Lem?"

"Yes. Go ahead."

"Who were the people who were killed?"

"If you tuned in late, what I said was that we intercepted the police calls concerning the murder scene and independently verified the report. We do have names which we know to be correct, but it would be irresponsible to release those names without their next of kin being notified. So give us a break, huh? A husband and wife and their two children were found murdered this morning, hacked to death, God rest their souls. The husband was a judge of elections. The motive for the murders seems obvious. Next caller. You're on the air."

"Lem?"

"Yes—go ahead, caller."

"This isn't a question, just a sort of statement."

"Go ahead—we have a thirty-second delay. I can take it."

"All right. If Roger Costigan wins, we'll put an end . . ."

There was a pause, then Lem Parrish's voice came back. "Hey. I hate to cut you off. Anybody who knows me knows with which candidate my sympathies lie, but we'll be getting into all sorts of hassles if you make a political endorsement. So let's just say that now is definitely a time for strong leadership. But whatever your political sentiments, you can really give the FLNA a good strong boot in the you-know-what by going out and voting. Next caller."

"This is the FLNA . . ."

There was the pause again.

Beside Holden, Rosie Shepherd sat bolt upright. "That's Johnson—I heard his voice in that truck stop—that's—"

Holden turned the volume as high as he could. Lem Parrish's voice came back on. "We've just recorded that caller's message. Normally, we wouldn't play it. But we just got a police report in that verifies the content. There's no way to authenticate it, but I think we're going to play it. I'll caution any of our listeners with delicate stomachs or young children nearby. This is pretty graphic. Here we go."

There was a pause, then Johnson's voice again. "This is the FLNA calling. The fascist pig oppressors of the people of North America will at last realize that they are not immune from the misery and suffering they have inflicted upon the masses for decades." There was no Russian accent; Holden had expected one. "An important operative in the Fascist Bureau of Investigation . . ." There was a pause, then Johnson/Borsoi continued: ". . . has been dealt the justice of the people. The scars she will carry on her face and body will serve as a reminder not only to her but to all who fight to preserve this rotting, pig government that the will of the people, which is justice, will prevail. It was not acid that was thrown at her—it was the tears of the oppressed peoples everywhere whom she has helped to keep enslaved. And what has happened to her will serve as a warning as well— Be on notice, all who would resist the will of the people. Your days are numbered, yours especially."

Lem Parrish's voice came back. "We deleted the woman's name, but she is an employee of the FBI— that's Federal Bureau of Investigation, of course, not what that idiot called it. Police reports we're getting indicate that some type of acid indeed was thrown into the woman's face, causing severe burns over her face and chest. But she is alive. It appears the FLNA has been keeping very busy with its reign of terror. If you are still listening, caller, I understand from your words that you're threatening me. Well, be on notice yourself. I can't call you what you are over the radio, but you know what I mean. Come on up to the radio station sometime and try threatening me to my face. And you'd better bring some friends because I spit out guys like you before breakfast. Remember, everybody—get out and vote!"

"Lem's gonna get himself killed or the radio station bombed," Rose Shepherd whispered. "Acid— Mother of God, what a thing to do. We need to talk with Pietrowski." It was starting to rain. David Holden started looking for a telephone booth. "Those fuckin' animals," Rosie hissed.

David Holden just looked at her, still held her. She buried her face against his shoulder for a little while. There was a convenience store/gas station at the brow of the hill and he figured they might risk the call from there. As he turned to tell Rosie his eyes were captured by her beautiful face, the skin so smooth, so soft to his touch. And inside his head he could see her face scarred and burned and gone. He turned in at the convenience store. The rain was coming down harder than he'd seen it in a long time.

CHAPTER 11

Clark Pietrowski had come in first. Luther Steel had left the underground facility almost a half hour later and received the transmission that something had happened to Anna Comacho when he was still several miles outside Metro.

She was hospitalized, at the same hospital where there'd been the shoot-out with the FLNA and he had first met Rosie Shepherd. Steel parked his F.O.U.O car illegally and entered through the emergency room, already knowing where Anna Comacho was being held—the intensive care unit.

As Steel stepped out of the elevator he could read it all in the faces of his men. Clark Pietrowski, Bill Runningdeer, Tom LeFleur, and the youngest of them, Randy Blumenthal. Steel started to ask who was minding the store but didn't bother; right now he didn't care.

Clark Pietrowski spoke first. "I've seen this shit before; the mob used to use it and—thank God for her that it was raining and she fell into the puddle. Or else it would have been worse. Hydrochloric acid, the doctors say. Jesus . . ."

"Why Miss Comacho?"

Luther Steel turned around and looked at Randy Blumenthal. "She's the one way to get to all of us, isn't she? Hitting our families would have been harder, required a lot more effort, manpower, and planning. And hitting us, well maybe they figured they might lose some of their own people. But hitting Anna—hell, I don't know."

58

"She's a tough kid," Pietrowski interjected. "She knew it was coming, couldn't get away from it, threw her hands in front of her face."

"How bad—"

"That's the doctor, Luther . . ." Pietrowski said it as he shoved past Steel, intercepting a green-coated man with a neatly trimmed beard and balding pate. Steel, Runningdeer, LeFleur, and Blumenthal fell in around Pietrowski.

"Who are you guys?" The doctor looked at each of them.

"We're her brothers," Steel hissed.

The doctor's eyes hardened for a minute, then he smiled. "FBI?"

Steel flashed his gold shield. It always worked better than the identity card.

"All right then." The doctor nodded. "She's in a bad way. There's some damage to her eyes—we have a specialist coming in as quickly as we can get him here. There's no telling the extent of damage to her skin— her face and neck and breasts, and especially her hands. Thank God for her that it was raining that heavily. . . ." Clark Pietrowski cleared his throat. "Otherwise, the effect of the acid would have been considerably worse. The only life-threatening situation we have will be her own will once she regains consciousness. There'll be the potential for considerable pain. We should be able to control that. We're checking her records with your Bureau for any allergic reactions, etc. But once she's aware of what happened to her—"

"What do you mean?" Luther Steel insisted.

"Look. I don't know this lady. You men evidently know her quite well. She's facing the substantial likelihood of serious, permanent disfigurement. Just from the look of her, it appears she was very beautiful."

Randy Blumenthal just repeated the word *was*.

There was the clicking sound of Clark Pietrowski's lighter and Steel smelled his cigarette smoke.

Bill Runningdeer said what they were all thinking. "The mother fuckers are gonna pay."

"Amen to that, Billy," Pietrowski murmured.

CHAPTER 12

It took a half hour to get through to Steel's office, and then the phone was answered by a secretary from the pool so it was impossible to leave a message, hanging up the only thing to do.

By the time they reentered the car, the rain still falling hard, both of them were soaked to the skin. Holden shut off the air-conditioning and rolled a window partway down, not driving away yet. "Give me a cigarette."

Rosie gave him one, lighting it first, her hands shaking. "She had a nice voice. I spoke to her the other day when we had to check something with Steel—"

"The Costigan raid thing." Holden nodded, inhaling the smoke as deep into his lungs as he could get it.

"I remember her answering with 'FBI Metro Task Force, Miss Comacho speaking'—something like that." Holden had been listening to the car radio while Rosie had kept trying to get the call through. Lem Parrish's station had broken the news that the injured woman was a secretary in the Special Task Force. Rosie had remembered the woman's name. Holden turned on the radio again. There was just music, one of the Beatles songs from their early days. As much as Holden liked it, he shut off the radio. He held Rosie's hands in his right hand, the cigarette in his left. "How could they do that? I mean, I knew they were scum—but . . ." There were tears in her eyes.

David Holden's voice was low as he spoke. "Listen—ah, why don't we reassess what we're doing. I

61

mean, you could just as easily . . ." It was the wrong time.

"What?"

"You could go somewhere safe and wait for me until this is all over."

There was determination in her eyes despite the tears as she looked up into his face. "And what happens if you get killed, David? Or what happens if this never gets over, at least not in our lifetimes? Huh? Then we both lose. Don't we?"

He pitched the cigarette through the open window into the rain, folding Rosie into his arms. "Yes," Holden whispered.

CHAPTER 13

They used the waiting room for a planning room, posting a sign reading "Closed" just outside, the corridor beyond clearly enough visible so there was no fear of eavesdropping. They had been allowed—all of them—to view Anna Comacho through one of those plexiglass windows hospitals sometimes use for isolation. Steel had seen his kids through windows like those.

Anna Comacho didn't have kids. She had an ex-husband who was in the middle of an important meeting and communicated through a secretary that he really didn't care what happened to Anna. Clark Pietrowski had made the call, nearly broken the receiver hanging up, sworn up and down, "Next time I'm out on the West Coast, that mother fucker's getting his butt kicked right into the damn Pacific Ocean."

Clark smoked. Randy looked more exhausted than anyone Steel had ever seen—he imagined it was the emotional drain—and Tom kept balling his fists. Bill Runningdeer paced. Luther Steel said, "Runningdeer and I are leaving this afternoon for Chicago. Mr. Cerillia's made arrangements for some discreet transportation into the city. If anybody stops in the office or calls, we're out on the streets running down leads on the attack on Anna. That's it. That includes the local police, anybody—especially the Bureau office in Chicago, as well as the regular Bureau people here. Considering that Mr. Cerillia's assistant, Tim Kjelstrom, was a plant, we don't know who else might be. And somebody had to know us pretty well to intercept Anna like that. Maybe things are still dirty."

"Boss?"

Steel looked at Pietrowski. "Yeah?"

"If you don't find anything incriminating in Chicago, then what?"

At first Steel had kept the true nature of the Special Task Force's mission a secret from everyone, its intended purpose to identify and contact the leader of the Patriot underground, David Holden, then convince Holden to ally with Director Cerillia and the President to coordinate efforts against the FLNA. That task accomplished, the second phase of their mission was already under way: by working with the Patriots and independently, they would attempt to crush the FLNA in Metro, by any reckoning a key piece in the FLNA's plans for the destruction of the United States Government. First, Clark Pietrowski had guessed the true nature of their mission, and soon after that Steel had confided in all the members of his Special Task Force. Including Anna Comacho. Director Cerillia was already preparing to have Anna transferred to a military hospital where she could be kept under constant guard and constant surveillance lest, in her pain, she say something incriminating.

Luther Steel answered Pietrowski's question. "We can't let Costigan win, can we? But we can't have him arrested on innuendo. We're up the creek if we don't find evidence in Chicago or somewhere. Which means we've got to find it."

He heard footsteps in the corridor, slipped his right hand under his jacket to the butt of the 66 2½ there.

What was coming down the corridor was worse than an enemy: it was Ralph Kaminsky, deputy commander of Metro PD.

"Here comes asshole," Pietrowski muttered.

Steel stood up. Runningdeer, nearest the door, looked at Steel quizzically. Steel shrugged. Runningdeer let Kaminsky pass. Two men were at Kaminsky's heels, both uniformed in SWAT gear. Kaminsky was using O'Brien's Metro SWAT team like his own personal honor guard. In the honor department, Steel thought, Kaminsky needed all the help he could get. "Mr. Kaminsky," Steel said, not smiling, not extending his hand.

"I'll get right to the point, Steel. What the hell are you and your Special Task Force up to that your secretary gets acid tossed in her face? Or what was she up to?"

Steel saw Pietrowski tense. Quickly, Steel said, "Just what do you mean?"

"Was she a target of revenge or did somebody just want her out of the way?"

"Revenge. That's what the clown said on the radio, wasn't it?"

"You think I believe the FLNA would bother calling a conservative bastard like Lem Parish and take credit for a thing like this?" Kaminsky laughed. "You must think I'm really stupid."

Steel couldn't help himself. It was the tension. It was the feeling of wanting to cry when he'd seen Anna Comacho's face and hands all bandaged and all the tubes leading in and out of her and not crying because he felt he shouldn't in front of the men. So he laughed.

"What's this?" Kaminsky snapped.

Steel shrugged his shoulders. "I was laughing because you really hit the nail on the head, for once. The FNLA could come up to you and bite you and you wouldn't believe they did it. Instead, you'd be off chasing law-abiding citizens for just trying to defend themselves. Yes, I think you're stupid. And the worst part of that is that this is still a fine police department here in Metro, one of the best in the nation. But what you're doing for their morale isn't helping it. We'll find the people who did this to Anna Comacho. If they can be arrested on federal charges—and that plaza is federal property—we'll do the arresting. If we can't get federal warrants, we'll turn them over to you."

"There's no sense talking to you—goes to show, I guess," Kaminsky snarled.

"Goes to show what, Mr. Kaminsky?" Steel pressed.

"Face it, man—for every one of you who lets ego get in the way . . ."

He'd expected the racial thing, he had heard about Kaminsky's treatment of blacks in Metro PD. He told Kaminsky, "Just get out of my sight—or this nigger's gonna turn your ass into Polish sausage, Kaminsky."

Kaminsky glared, turned around, and walked out.

Luther Steel realized his hands were shaking. It was only a matter of time before he totally lost his temper and decked Ralph Kaminsky—which would look very bad.

He looked at his men, saying, "Special Agent Pietrowski's in charge of the Task Force while I'm away. And especially if Kaminsky asks—"

Pietrowski laughed. "Luther who?"

CHAPTER 14

The French Impressionist paintings still intrigued him. Humphrey Hodges asked, "Why did you do that horrible thing, Mr. Johnson?" They were forgeries, of course. It was impossible to conceive of Humphrey Hodges owning anything that was valuable.

"What horrible thing, Hodges?" He stood up and walked over to the bookcase. If it had not been locked, he would have opened it. Although the books inside looked to be genuine first editions, Borsoi wondered. "Are these real?" Borsoi finally asked.

"I'm talking about something that may have ruined our chances to win the election—heaven only knows the polls are terribly disappointing—and you talk about—"

"Are these real?" Borsoi insisted.

"Yes."

"How did you come by them?"

"What?" Hodges asked, almost sounding as though he weren't paying attention. "How did I come by them?"

"Yes. Where did you get that kind of money?"

"I—well—my wife, God rest her soul—she was—"

Borsoi looked Humphrey Hodges square in the eye, asking, "Did you kill her for them? Or for money?"

Hodges gasped.

Borsoi laughed aloud. "Only if you poisoned her or something, Hodges. Do not worry. You could not kill anyone who was looking at you or whom you thought might fight back. And don't tell me how to run my people. You'll remember, I am in charge here and you work for me. This political campaign is going exactly as I wish it to—because I wish it to."

"Then you do support Costigan!"

"Bravo, Hodges! How many nights did you stay awake figuring that out, hmm? Why else is Costigan alive? If I'd wanted Costigan dead, feared Costigan's election, he would have been dead." And he smiled at Hodges, adding, "Anyone who stands in my way does not stand there for long."

"Then the woman," Hodges began. "She was—"

"She was a very useful person, this Anna Comacho. The incident sent a message to Steel and his Task Force. And it sent a message to the hard-core, America-right-or-wrong voters—everything is out of control, totally. You must, somehow, vote for Costigan to defeat these evil forces of the FLNA. Just what I want."

Hodges stood up, sat down again, leaned across his desk, looked almost totally disoriented. "But how—how could you own Roger Costigan?"

Borsoi smiled. He very much wanted to tell Hodges, to watch the reaction in Hodges's watery eyes, but to tell Hodges the secret would be to give Hodges power, and Hodges was not a man to trust with power because he had no will to wield it and through his inabilities could do much harm. "Suffice it to say, I do. You came to me out of conviction; I suppose I should respect that, and perhaps, in a way, I do. Which is why I've let you work with me. Costigan's only concerns are personal. And he is very useful to us, not merely in Metro, not merely as the overwhelming choice of the voters for mayor, but useful to us nationally as well. I could dispense with him less easily than I could dispense with you. Do you have any more of that sherry I had the last time I was in your office?" And Borsoi began looking around for the decanter. . . .

The rain was still falling heavily. David Holden had always liked rain. But with only a two-man tent for shelter, rain could be a problem, especially as rapidly as it was falling now. Rain was also a problem when fighting a battle, and a battle was planned for tonight. With heavy rain, the enemy's response level would be down. They wouldn't expect anyone to attack.

He watched Rosie as she sat with her bare legs crossed and brushed her auburn hair. She was always pretty, sometimes unbelievably pretty, and this was one of those times.

"What are you looking at?"

"I'm watching you brush your hair. It turns me on."

"Right."

"No—I mean it. A woman couldn't understand."

She looked at him, said what he knew he'd set himself up for. "Did . . . ah . . . did you . . . Forget it."

"Did I watch Liz brush her hair? Yes," he told her. His wife's hair had been beautiful. It was hard to think of her as past, gone. Rosie in his present didn't make that any easier, but made everything else easier. "I watched my wife whenever I could. I remember little things. Like how she held a knife all wrong when she'd peel a potato or something. Things like that. I realized something a little while ago, though. Love isn't quantitative. It's qualitative only. The time doesn't make any difference to the quality, how little or how much time. It's who you're with." He knelt up beside her, drew her into his arms, brought his mouth down hard on hers, and held her so tightly, he was afraid he'd crush her.

CHAPTER 15

Each step David Holden took buried his feet in mud to his ankles. There was a sucking sound as he lifted each foot for the next step. The rain, driven now on a hard wind, felt almost cool to exposed skin, made everything look slick and new. But beneath the rain poncho he wore, David Holden's flesh crawled with rivulets of sweat. He was nearly as wet beneath the GI poncho as he would have been without it.

He caught a glimpse of Rosie Shepherd helping Patsy Alfredi and Helen Swensen. Patsy and Helen had volunteered themselves as the machine-gun team. Holden hoped to use the captured M-60 against the FLNA if they attempted to escape. He slogged toward the three women, slinging his M-16 across his back and addressing all of them as he took the machine gun: "Here, give me that." Between the gun itself and the extra barrel and the ammo cans of link-belt 7.62mm NATO rounds, carrying the gun into position through the mud seemed an impossible task for the two women and Rosie was already burdened enough.

With the muzzle pointed downward to minimize rain intake, he kept going, Rosie beside him now as they started over the next low hill. "That was nice of you to do that," she told him over the cacophony of rain and wind and slapping footfalls.

"Thanks for noticing." He smiled.

Beyond the next hill lay a flat expanse of meadow. It was low ground and would be even harder to traverse. Beyond the meadow lay a parking lot, a low, basic, chain link fence describing its perimeter on three

70

sides. On the fourth side lay Aviteck Electronics, Aviteck a once-flourishing business but in the last month forced to close because the company could get no workers to take the third shift and hence could not meet obligations. The Aviteck plant building, abandoned, in the last two weeks had become a storage depot for the FLNA. The loss of the arms and ammunition stored there would be a serious blow to the FLNA's campaign of violence against the Metro electorate. Aviteck's de facto takeover was the final proof that connected the police chief of the small town of Blackwood to the FLNA. There had been rumors since Holden had first become involved with the Patriots, and several members had argued that something should be done about Blackwood's top cop. Holden was not in the assassination business, but Aviteck's abandoned plant site being an almost open FLNA facility was the conclusive proof of collusion. Almost absently Holden wondered what sort of hold the FLNA had over the man. Or was he simply a Communist sympathizer or some other variant of misguided left-winger?

They began the descent into the defile between this hill and the next, water raging in torrents through eroded gullies in the low ground, the footing looking treacherous.

It proved to be.

Pedro "Pete" Villalobos went down, Mimi Baker laughing at his misfortune, then falling into the water herself, both of them laughing at each other. It was good to see them laugh, despite the circumstances. The Patriots kept going, up the next hill. As the M-60 got heavier Rosie convinced Holden to put it down for a moment, relieved him of his M-16, and carried the assault rifle for him.

At the brow of the final hill they stopped.

His people formed around him. Holden rested the butt of the M-60 in the mud beside his feet. "Let's go over it quick. Helen and Patsy—set up the machine gun by the parking-lot gates in that stand of pines right beside the Aviteck sign near the driveway. The sign's concrete and should give you good cover if it gets to that. Pete—you and your people help Patsy and Helen get the gun into position, then take up your positions on both sides of the driveway and along the front of the building." Holden looked at Larry Perkins, Perkins towering over almost everyone in the group, taller than Holden as well. "Larry—your people have the rear entrance by the loading dock and the back side of the parking lot. Rosie and I'll lead our people in, neutralize as many as we can, and plant the explosives. As soon as you see us out the door, use those radio detonators Mitch Diamond rigged up, and Aviteck's history. If you don't see us out in twenty minutes, we won't be coming out, so detonate everything you've got."

"I still don't like that," Perkins drawled. "What if you bump into resistance and just can't move in or out?"

"One of us will get out or get to you on the radio. So relax on that part, okay?"

"I don't like it—but yeah." Perkins nodded.

Holden looked at Rosie, then at the others. "Let's do it, guys," he said, then caught up the machine gun and handed it into Pete Villalobos's sodden arms. . . .

The chief's car was in the Aviteck parking lot near the loading docks. Brazen wasn't the word for it, Holden thought. And if the small town's traitorous police chief was inside, it might well be his last opportunity to betray the public trust.

Crossing the fence was easy, Holden, Rosie Shepherd, and four other Patriots making the initial penetration to neutralize what human security there might be. Intelligence indicated that one man was stationed inside the facility's front entrance at the security station, although the cameras were inoperable. Two men were stationed on the loading dock at the rear, and occasionally there was a fourth man who would wander the grounds. Holden doubted the fourth man was out tonight but wasn't willing to bet on it.

Across the parking lot, feeling awkward in the rain gear, covering the front and rear of the parking lot with their M-16s as they looked for the fourth man, they ran as quickly as they could to reach the near wall of the building. The rain drove down on them in torrents so intense that it was almost impossible to see.

Holden sagged against the wall surface, Rosie beside him, the other four Patriots at the wall now too.

Holden signaled them to move on, keeping as close to the wall as he could.

The building was a single story, with large vented windows as vestiges of it prior use as a textile plant. At the end of the wall Holden stopped. He looked at Rosie Shepherd. Rainwater cascaded from the lip of her hood as she made a last-minute check of her M-16. Holden reached beneath his poncho and drew the Defender knife.

He edged to the corner and peered around the other side. He could see the near end of the loading dock. No one was in sight. Again Holden reached beneath his poncho, to his left hip, where he carried the larger of his two 92F series Berettas, and drew it cavalry style from the Bianchi UM-84 holster. He signaled to the four other Patriots as he and Rosie slipped around the corner, Rosie's M-16 at an almost unnaturally high port, Holden's knife in a rapier hold near his right shoulder, the full-sized Beretta military pistol balled tightly in his left fist.

The rain lashed at them.

They reached the end of the loading dock. The 9mm pistol and the Crain Defender knife still in his hands, Holden shoved himself up and onto the loading dock. There was a yellow light visible beyond the swinging flexible doors, which were like huge mud flaps, with a semirigid transparent opening at about head height.

Rosie clambered onto the loading dock, keeping in a low crouch as she crossed to the far side of the doors. Holden signaled the four other Patriots to close on the loading dock. He took up a position on the near side of the doors. Rosie held the M-16 bisecting her body from the right side of her waist upward beyond her left shoulder and the left side of her neck. She pushed the hood back from her hair and nodded.

Holden nodded back.

Rosie took a step toward the doors and kicked the one nearest her.

She stepped back.

On a night like this it could have been a strong gust of wind, but even the most unwilling sentry would check—Holden hoped.

The door near him opened slightly. Holden moved the knife in his fingers, into a dagger hold.

A man stepped through, face twisted against the wind and rain, an Uzi submachine gun in his right fist. As he stepped through Holden stepped forward, the pistol in his left fist hammering downward against the base of the man's skull as Holden's right drove downward to the apex of the triangle formed by the right shoulder and the right side of the neck. The Uzi fell from limp fingers, swinging on its sling beneath the man's right arm. The body sagged forward, Holden released the knife, already buried half to the hilt, and grabbing for the man, Holden dragged him back toward the edge of the loading dock.

Holden rolled the body over into the waiting arms of two of his men, tearing his knife free as he let go.

Holden looked at Rosie Shepherd. She was standing on her toes, peering through the transparent opening in the far side door. She held up one finger, gestured toward Holden's side of the loading dock, then pantomimed a sitting position. She gripped the rifle again as she had before. She nodded that she was ready.

Holden nodded back, tightened his fist on his pistol, rolled the Crain knife into a rapier hold, and went through.

One man, in his late teens or early twenties, a cigarette hanging from the right side of a slack-jawed mouth, sat slouched in a chair, a can of beer on the table nearer to him than his Uzi. As he tried to stand and reach for the submachine gun at the same time, Holden crossed toward him in three long steps, lunged with the Defender knife, and impaled the man through the throat, nearly upsetting the table. Holden, balancing the table against his right hip as he caught the body up near him, twisted the knife once and the body went limp—dead.

Holden eased the body to the floor, leaving the knife in place as he grabbed up the Uzi in his right fist, the Beretta in his left hand already sweeping the area surrounding the table. He saw a few innocuous-looking boxes and a few cases of beer, probably stolen. There was a clear field of view up to the doors at the far end, and there was no one in sight. He took off the M-16, leaned it against the table.

It was suffocatingly warm. Holden set down the Uzi, and as he started to strip off his poncho, Rosie came through between the doors. He moved the muzzle of the Beretta toward her and she winked back. He finished with the poncho, throwing it across the table, reholstering the Beretta 92F. Rosie disappeared through the doors again, returning a second later followed by the first of the four Patriots.

Holden handed the Uzi to one of the men as he picked up the M-16. Already the four Patriots were shrugging out of their packs, which contained the explosives. Rosie was out of her poncho, throwing it onto the table beside his.

Together, on opposite sides of the corridor formed by the building's support posts, David Holden and Rosie Shepherd moved toward the doors at the far end of the loading area. Already, Holden was worried that they had struck too late. Where were the crates of arms, ammunition, explosives?

They crept up to the doors.

CHAPTER 16

The airfield in the far northern Chicago suburbs was all but abandoned, a single-engine Cessna parked near the hangars at the far end, nothing else in evidence. The pilot of the twin-engine Beechcraft jet was Director Cerillia's choice when he had to fly—and Cerillia flew only when it was unavoidable. The pilot had noted to Steel and Runningdeer, the only passengers, that they were coming in totally on their own. The tower wasn't staffed. There were no electronic navigational aids in operation.

As Luther Steel and Bill Runningdeer stepped out onto the tarmac, Runningdeer murmured, "Thank God we made it."

Steel laughed, telling him, "You've been hanging around Mr. Cerillia too much; you're getting his fear of flying. I didn't know that sort of thing was contagious."

"Yeah, well maybe it is, Luther." The tall American Indian FBI agent smiled. "I guess that's our car."

Luther Steel looked along the runway and down toward where the little white Cessna was parked. The dark sedan was rolling steadily toward them. "Help the pilot with our luggage, Bill."

"Right, boss."

Steel and Runningdeer had one small suitcase each, a suit bag shared between them. Luther Steel stretched his hands over his head. He brought his hands down to his hips, sweeping his coattails back, waiting as the sedan approached. The windshield glass was very dark and he couldn't see inside.

Something started knotting up in his stomach.

Without taking his eyes off the black sedan, he called over his shoulder to Runningdeer, "Hey, Bill. Check out the sedan!"

The sedan was closer than a hundred yards now.

Its bright lights came on suddenly, and would have momentarily blinded him with their brilliance if a mosquito hadn't buzzed him and he looked away to swat at it. "Bill! Get the pilot down!" Steel hit the tarmac, drawing the Sig-Sauer P-226 as he rolled, the runway surface splintering beside him as he heard the blast of the shotgun, then heard it again and again, the shotgun almost drowned out in the roar of the submachine gun. There was just one long burst, whole chunks of runway surface spraying upward, bullets pinging off the aircraft's fuselage.

Steel stabbed the Sig toward the sedan and fired as fast as he could pull the trigger. Quickly he was on his feet, running as he made a tactical magazine change, going to one of the two twenty-round spares he carried, thumbing down the slide stop and letting the slide slam forward as a fresh fusillade of automatic weapons fire poured from the passenger side of the sedan.

"Heads up, Luther!" Bill Runningdeer was running diagonally across the tarmac, the Uzi they'd brought, which was Runningdeer's pet weapon, spraying neat little bursts of fire across the distance separating him from the black sedan.

The sedan's headlights went out on the passenger side; one was already out on the driver's side. Steel mentally patted himself on the back that he'd hit something when he'd dumped the first magazine. Luther Steel brought the Sig into a point shoulder position in both fists as he knelt beside the Beechcraft's landing gear. He fired, aiming for the darkness of the passenger-side seats, the darkness continually punctuated with muzzle flashes. He fired a two-round burst, then another and another and another. The vehicle swerved, started turning around. Runningdeer was firing from a ditch at the right side of the runway in neat bursts, blowing out the sedan's right front tire.

Luther Steel was up, the Sig transferred into his left fist, his right hand tearing the little Smith & Wesson revolver from under his left shoulder. A pistol in each hand, he ran toward the vehicle, spraying both handguns toward the darkness of the passenger side. An object fell from the front seat to the runway surface as the sedan screeched through a bootlegger turn and accelerated away. At first Steel thought it might be some sort of explosive device. As he closed with it he realized it was a submachine gun. He'd hit somebody. From the direction of the ditch he could hear Runningdeer emptying the Uzi toward the fast-accelerating auto.

Steel lowered his handguns, six rounds still in the Sig, the Smith revolver empty.

Runningdeer was beside him. "Somebody knew we were coming," Runningdeer noted superfluously.

"Or somebody knew to expect us—maybe Costigan." Steel cleared his throat. "How's the pilot?"

"Fine, I think."

"Go check him out," Steel ordered. As he looked down at his blue blazer and gray slacks, then at Runningdeer's khaki suit, Steel added, "Good thing we brought a change of clothes, huh?"

"Good thing we brought plenty of ammunition too," Runningdeer said, jogging off toward the pilot.

Steel picked up the submachine gun that had fallen from the sedan. "I bet you're stolen from some arsenal, baby," he murmured.

CHAPTER 17

Holden moved along the wide corridor beyond the interior doors, Rosie Shepherd behind him, both of them hugging the wall as they moved. He heard a noise behind him, looked back, and saw the four Patriots coming, broken into two two-man teams to plant the explosives.

The corridor split right and left and a staircase continued upward ahead. The left corridor right-angled abruptly about twenty yards along its length, both corridors leading toward the front of the building. Holden signaled the two teams, one to each corridor. He looked at Rosie Shepherd and nodded toward the staircase.

Holden and Rosie Shepherd took the staircase almost back to back, Holden in the lead, shifting the M-16 to his left fist, drawing the Desert Eagle .44 into his right. If somebody suddenly loomed in their path, he wanted that somebody down for the count quickly. Holden glanced back once. Rosie moved behind him, taking the stairs backwards, her M-16 shifting from side to side, covering the entire base of the stairwell.

They neared the top of the staircase. The single-story appearance from the outside was only partially deceptive, the second floor a small superstructure added over the main building, perhaps three thousand square feet at best compared to the quarter million square feet of the Aviteck factory itself.

Holden took the right side of the stairwell, Rosie Shepherd the left. They paused, listening. Holden heard voices. The FLNA sympathizer Blackwood police chief perhaps? He almost hoped so.

The voices came from the right. Holden nodded toward the sound, Rosie signaled that she heard the voices too. She indicated with her left hand that she would cross the corridor at the head of the stairs toward an open doorway (some sort of office) just opposite the stairs.

Holden signaled that she should wait, inched upward, prone against the stair treads, peering down to his left, looking for any sign of activity. Nothing but shadows and what might have been some sort of storage room or executive washrooms there.

He looked to his right. There was an office at the far side of the superstructure, the frosted-glass-panel door open, a wide, watery shaft of yellow-tinged light emanating from inside. He could still hear the voices. He pushed himself up, cramped his feet onto the top tread, the M-16 beside his left thigh, finger in the trigger guard and the selector on auto, the Desert Eagle .44 tight in his right fist, hammer cocked, safety off. He gave Rosie a nod and she sprinted across the corridor, molding into the shadows of the darkened office door.

She peered out, nodded, and Holden slipped around the corner, in plain view if anyone should look from the lighted office. As he started moving forward no one looked.

The voices were clearer now! ". . . the hell anybody says. Not even the federal boys will move in my town without me knowing it. I've got enough connections," the older-sounding voice concluded. The collaborator police chief of Blackwood? Probably, Holden thought.

A voice with an unidentifiable foreign accent replied, "This place is too exposed, I think. We should have had everything out of here and into the right hands a week ago or better. And there should be more guards on duty, I think."

Then a third voice, unaccented, young-sounding: "Look, guys, we've got those trucks comin' in about fifteen minutes . . ." Holden looked at his watch. Eight minutes into the mission. Twelve to get out before the explosives were detonated. Could a fortunate bit of timing be pulled off? ". . . and then all our problems are over, huh? So relax. You want more guards, Muli, fine, Chief Helbrose and me'll go walk around, all right? You can come to."

Holden and Rosie were flanking the office door. Holden heard a chair scrape against the floor.

Their eyes met.

Holden gestured with the Desert Eagle.

Rosie Shepherd reached for the adopted Glock from one of the two holsters on her hips, taking a step back, her M-16 and the Glock 17 leveled at the doorway.

The first man through the doorway had to be the one called Muli. He was swarthy, wore expensive casual clothes, and held a Uzi submachine gun in his hands as though he knew how to use one.

Rose Shepherd snapped, "Freeze!"

Somebody yelled, "Shit!"

Muli swung the muzzle of the Uzi toward Rosie. Holden shot Muli twice with the Desert Eagle, the first round in the chest, the second round in the neck as the pistol rose slightly in recoil. There was blood all over the wall beside the office door. Muli's head snapped back into the glass and the glass shattered. A young-looking man with a pearl-gripped, bright chrome-plate or polished stainless-steel .45 automatic stuffed in the front of high-waisted dress pants and an identical-looking .45 in his right hand opened fire, Rosie shooting him in the chest with the M-16, Holden dodging back to stay out of her line of fire, putting one into the younger man's left shoulder with the Desert Eagle.

Holden saw a blur and felt something strike his head, and as he stumbled he heard Rosie Shepherd shrieking, "Dammit—it's the crooked cop!"

Holden was on his knees, seeing a figure darting down the corridor toward the stairwell. He stabbed the M-16 after him and fired a long burst, chunks of wall board disintegrating under it, a streak of blood along the wall, the chief—Helbrose—disappearing down the stairwell. Holden looked for Rosie. The young guy with the fancy .45s was on top of her and she was shoving his body away. "Son of a bitch threw this joker against me," she hissed. "He hit you with that," she said, getting to her feet at last. Holden, still on his knees, looked where Rosie pointed. There was a piece of granite with words engraved into the base. Its shape looked familiar. "I'm goin' after him—you all right?"

Holden slumped back against the wall, seeing stars. "Yeah—be careful!" Holden added as Rosie Shepherd ran past him. He looked at the object again. "Plymouth Rock—1620." He tried to stand up, felt something warm and moist trickling down along the right side of his face and saw more stars. . . .

Rosie Shepherd fired out her M-16 into the base of the stairwell, then ran for it, the Glock in her left fist. By the time she hit the base of the stairs, the M-16—empty—hung at her right side on its sling and the blackened Detonics Servicemaster .45 was in her right hand. She tried analyzing the blur of motion she'd seen. A tall man, overweight, a pistol on his right hip. He was even wearing his uniform.

There was more blood by the base of the stairs. David had nailed him. But how seriously? she wondered.

"Yo—Helbrose! Give it up, man!" She clung to the shadows at the base of the stairs, listening.

"Fuck you!"

"In your dreams!" Rosie shouted back. He was off to her right. That was where the corridor went on for twenty yards or so and then right-angled toward the front of the building. There was a team there, planting explosives. She looked at her watch. Six minutes until the explosives would be detonated. She could get David, help him outside, then let the crooked cop get blown up along with the building. But if the two Patriots laying the explosives on that end of the building stumbled into him, there could be needless bloodshed or they would be trapped inside.

Rosie Shepherd edged into the hallway, the pistols close at her sides, ready. It was only in movies where cops postured around like ballet dancers with their guns stuck out a yard ahead of them.

She kept moving.

"You a cop? Look. I can make a deal. Plenty of money, for you and the guy too. He'll be okay. Just hit him with a damn paperweight."

She didn't answer.

She almost felt the movement around the corner of the corridor, whatever subtle visual cue it was that had alerted her lost in the jumble of her thoughts and reflexes as Chief Helbrose stomped his right foot into the corridor, his revolver—maybe it had been the brightness of the nickel plating she had seen—in his right hand, his body in the classic FBI gunfighting crouch of decades ago. He fired it. It had to be a .357 Magnum, the sound and the muzzle flash just about right for that but not ear-splitting enough for a .44 like David used.

He missed.

Rose Shepherd fired both pistols simultaneously, Helbrose's body rocking with the multiple impacts, slamming against the wall, crumpling, dark wet streaks trailing along the wall after him.

Rose Shepherd stopped shooting, the Servicemaster empty of all seven shots, the Glock down to maybe a dozen.

She approached him, the Glock just slightly ahead of her body. His hand still held the revolver. She kicked it away and stepped back.

He wasn't moving, which meant he was either dead or naturally good at playing statue. And he didn't look like the gamesman type. Rose Shepherd snarled, "That's for the honest cops, scum."

CHAPTER 18

Men were moving out of the main work area of the factory and there was gunfire everywhere, nearly two dozen FLNA personnel that Holden had counted from the stairwell flooding through the doors toward the storage area abutting the loading dock. Larry Perkins and the Patriots with him wouldn't open fire because the demolitions teams were still inside. Rosie Shepherd's hands were shaking when he joined her in the right-angle corridor at the base of the stairs. He knew her better than to think it was fear. When he saw the dead body of the collaborator police chief, he knew her hands trembled with rage. She was a cop's kid. She would still have been a cop herself if a solid, basic sense of right and wrong hadn't brought her into the Patriots with Rufus Burroughs. Holden's mind flashed to Burroughs for an instant. Police sergeant, veteran, the original leader of the Metro Patriots and one of the chief organizers of the Patriot movement nationwide. Dead after leading a raid against the FLNA to prevent their precipitating a meltdown at a nuclear power facility that could have killed or contaminated thousands. The Desert Eagle .44 in Holden's right fist had been Rufus Burroughs's gun. Holden safed the pistol now, secured it in the Southwind Sanctions SAS holster at his right thigh. "You all right?"

"How about you?" Rosie asked, loading a fresh magazine into her .45.

"Got a headache and feel like a fool. Other than that . . . What's all the gunfire? Our people in trouble, you think?"

"Yeah." She nodded. "How much time we got?"

"Three minutes," Holden said, consulting the Rolex on his left wrist.

"Will Larry detonate like you ordered him to?"

"Probably. Better get our people and boogie, huh? In case we can't get out that fast, I'll try raising him on the radio." And Holden grinned at her. "You take this end, I'll take the other. Don't either one of us wait for the other, right?"

"Bullshit. You know I'll wait and I know you'll wait. So we'd better quit gabbing." She rammed a magazine into her M-16, then leaned up on her toes and kissed him quick on the mouth, peered around the bend, then ran off down the corridor.

Holden's head seemed to vibrate with each step, but he ran anyway, retracing his steps past the stairwell, turning off into the other corridor after checking that it was clear. The gunfire inside the building seemed to be falling off. Some machinery was still in place from the Aviteck operation, but much of it was moved aside, some of it upended, and crates with United States Government markings were visible everywhere as he came out of the short corridor and into the main floor of the factory. He could see Rosie on the other side. But there was no time to call to her. There was a pocket of gunfire toward the front end of the factory. Holden took out his radio from a pocket of his Kevlar fitted battle vest. "Larry—you reading me? This is David. Over."

"Reading you loud and clear, David. Talk to me. Over."

"This place is emptying out. There's a little firefight going on toward the front of the factory. Rosie's closing in from one side, I'm taking the other in a second. There should be some trucks pulling up in a couple of minutes to haul off the stuff in here. If we can swing it, let's take those trucks. Get word to Patsy

if she isn't monitoring this. Tell her to let the trucks in
if they show up but not to let them out. Save the
demolitions until we have to. Maybe we can hijack the
trucks and use some of this stuff ourselves. Looks like
M-16s, 1911A1s"—he pulled back a tarp, looked at two
crates beneath it—"maybe some Beretta M-9s. And
ammo for everything. Some LAW Rockets too. What
about the FLNA-ers splitting the factory? Over."

"They're in the parking lot. Nobody opened up on
them yet, and that business with the trucks makes
sense. They must be waitin' for the trucks. Over."

"Can you handle my suggestions? Over."

"Is 'roger' the right thing to say or 'wilco'? Over."

Holden felt himself smile. "You should say 'wilco'
when you will comply and 'roger' to indicate the message is understood. Out."

He pouched the radio, then started forward,
threading his way through the stacks of packing crates
and abandoned manufacturing equipment toward the
gun battle at the front of the factory. Holden could no
longer see Rosie Shepherd. . . .

Rose Shepherd drew the Cold Steel Tanto, the
mini-Tanto strapped to her leg beneath her BDU pants,
the full-sized Tanto on her belt. With the larger knife
she pried open the crate beside which she knelt. It
held what David called "M-67 time-delay fragmenta-
tion grenades" and she'd always called "baseball grenades," which seemed a lot simpler to say and seemed
much more descriptive. She resheathed her knife and
moved aside the packing material. She took one of the
grenades out. As a cop she had very little opportunity
to learn about grenades aside from watching guys like
Chuck Norris or Arnold Schwarzenegger toss them at
bad guys in the movies. But Rufus Burroughs had told
her about them. She'd never noticed it in the movies,

but there were actually two safety devices on this type of grenade.

The first was the usual split-ring/cotter-pin affair that John Wayne always pulled out with his teeth. The second was a little wire clip that would hold the lever, or "spoon" as David called it, down in place even with the pin withdrawn. If somebody was going into battle, the grenades expected to be used on an immediate basis might have the little wire clips removed so that all that was necessary was to pull the pin, figure how long to hold on to it before throwing (since they had a maximum of five seconds delay time, holding on to one too long wasn't advisable), then toss it.

She wondered how much the FLNA bad guys knew about M-67s? And how sharp-eyed they might be?

She experimented, the gunfire regular but not spectacular in the nearby firefight, pulling the pin, gently releasing hand pressure against the spoon. Nothing happened. She smiled. . . .

David Holden crept along the row of crates nearest to the FLNA position. One of the four Patriots was down, dead or wounded, another was stiff-armed but still returning fire, meaning non-life-threatening wound. The other two were alternating between their M-16s and pistols.

There were at least a dozen FLNA personnel.

Where was Rosie?

Holden kept moving at a right angle to the FLNA position. His M-16 tight in both fists, Holden raised to a standing position and fired, spraying into the dozen FLNA-ers, then throwing himself right into a nest of tarps as gunfire hammered back toward him. He stabbed the Desert Eagle over his cover, meager as it was, fired two shots, then ran, gunfire tearing into the packing crates. If he could make them think that a substantial force outflanked them—

"Hey—FLNA!" It was Rosie's voice. "Throw down your weapons or we all die together! Figure what a grenade would do with all this stuff around in a confined area like this. Figure what a whole bunch of grenades would do!"

"Grenades?" Holden verbalized. Was she crazy?

"Got ten seconds. Nine seconds. Eight. Seven. You got six." Holden put a fresh magazine up the well of the M-16, ready to back Rosie's play even if it did seem insane. "Five seconds—the hell with it; I'm tired of counting!" Holden caught the arc of the first grenade as a blur at the far left corner of his peripheral vision. He knew she liked softball, was good at it—but did she realize what she was doing? Then another grenade and another and another and another.

The FLNA-ers started to bolt from their positions, Holden shouting, "Rosie! Take cover!" as he threw himself down behind what protection he could find and opened fire, spraying into them, gunfire spitting from where he approximated Rosie's position to be, catching the FLNA-ers in a devastating crossfire. All of them were down within fifteen seconds.

"Fifteen seconds," Holden mused aloud, waiting for the explosions one after the other. But they would have already happened.

He looked toward Rosie's position. She laughed, her rifle balanced on the buttstock against her right hip, legs wide apart, her hair tossed back over her shoulders. "Wanna help me put the pins back in?"

David Holden breathed. . . .

The rain still poured down.

David Holden, Rosie Shepherd, and the two unscathed Patriots waited beside the loading dock. The less seriously wounded Patriot was farther back into the building, taking care of the more seriously wounded man.

The FLNA-ers who had escaped the building were forming up for an attack in the parking lot.

Holden heard the grinding of a truck transmission from the entrance. Then another. Then another. There was enough in the Aviteck factory for six trucks at least, if he had gauged it right.

He could just see the bullet nose of the first cab. FLNA-ers were congregating around it. Holden spoke into the radio. "How we doing, Patsy? Over."

Patsy Alfredi's voice came back. "Three eighteen-wheelers in the lot. They won't get back out unless we let 'em. Over."

"Pete—talk to me. Over."

"David—we're ready. Over."

"Larry? You ready? Over."

"On your signal, David. Over."

"Everybody stand by," Holden hissed. The FLNA-ers were forming a skirmishing line, the truck Holden had seen inching ahead, the men falling in with the truck between them and the loading dock, still unaware, it seemed, of Perkins's people, who would have them in plain view. Rosie was in a prone position, her rifle to her shoulder, a second beside her. The two other Patriots on the loading dock were ready as well. "On three, folks," Holden whispered, loudly enough that Rosie and the two Patriots with them would hear. "One . . . two . . . three! Let 'em have it!" Holden put down the radio and started shooting, gunfire already pouring into the parking lot from Perkins's men in position beyond the rear of the building.

The FLNA line behind the truck broke, the truck sped up, and the FLNA-ers ran toward the front of the parking lot. "Moving your way, Pete, Patsy! Larry—you and your guys close in from the rear and stop those trucks if they try to punch through the fence. Holden, out." David Holden, Rosie beside him, jumped from the loading dock into the rain-puddled parking lot, the rain falling more heavily than before.

Holden ran, Rosie sprinting along beside him, fleeing FLNA-ers swapping shots over their shoulders as they ran for the front parking-lot gate.

Holden had his M-16 fired out, rammed a fresh magazine up the well, began firing again, still running.

FLNA-ers were going down.

Holden jumped over a body. A burst of gunfire tore out chunks of brick in the wall near him and he averted his eyes from the dust spray. Rosie shot a man trying to jump onto the running board of one of the trucks. The truck driver stepped out, a shotgun in his hands. Holden emptied the M-16 into him and the body fell away.

Holden, carrying one of the Beretta pistols in each hand, let the rifle fall to his side on its sling.

At the far edge of his peripheral vision he could see one of the two remaining trucks stopped, the driver surrendering to Larry Perkins's unit.

The third truck was backing toward the front gate.

Patsy Alfredi and Helen Swensen opened up with the M-60 machine gun. The truck skidded, fishtailed, started forward. A knot of four FLNA-ers charged toward Holden and Rosie Shepherd, Rosie emptying her M-16 of its last three or four rounds, firing her Glock pistol. Holden turned toward them, the Berettas in both fists pulsing.

"David! Look out!" He barely heard her voice as he wheeled around. The eighteen-wheeler that had tried backing out the front gate was bearing down on him, fewer than twenty yards away, picking up speed, its engine roaring in low gear. At the far right edge of his peripheral vision Holden saw the muzzle flashes as Rosie emptied the Glock.

The truck was still coming. David Holden's

thumbs worked down the safeties, his hands ramming the Berettas into his pistol belt, his right hand sweeping to his side, his right thumb hitting the safety, his right arm punching forward into the cup formed by his left hand, the Desert Eagle .44 Magnum rocking in his fists, tongues of yellow and orange flame almost obliterating the truck from view.

He emptied the magazine, stepped right, and ran, the truck missing him by inches. He wheeled back toward it as he started into a fast tactical magazine change with the Desert Eagle, using the spare magazine pouched on the Southwind Sanctions holster. But the truck seemed to lurch, skidded, the cab overturning, the trailer jackknifing. Holden shouted, "Rosie! Run for it!" He didn't quite know what he'd hit, but he'd aimed for the radiator, hoping to punch through into the fan.

The trailer was snapping over on its left side, the cab skidding, steam belching from the radiator, then a flicker of flame shot out from where the carburetor would be. Holden ran, grabbed Rosie by the left arm, dragged her with him, throwing her down, the Desert Eagle still in his right fist. His body was over hers as there was a loud rushing sound like wind, then his ears rang and a wave of heat suddenly washed across his rain-drenched body.

When the wave had passed he slowly raised his face, looked back, Rosie edging out from beneath him, coming to her knees beside him. The truck was engulfed in flames. Whatever its mission, it hadn't been empty coming into the Aviteck parking lot. The cargo had exploded.

There was a smell like rotten eggs only worse, and Holden was starting to feel light-headed.

He dragged Rosie to her feet. She sagged against him. The smoke from the fire billowed upward. "Evacuate!" Holden shouted into his radio. "Hazardous chemicals in the truck. Evacuate! Larry—if you're reading me, count to ten slowly and then hit those detonators. Run for it! Everybody! Move! Move!"

He needed to catch Rosie up in his arms. She was starting to pass out. It was the radio or the Desert Eagle. Mitch Diamond had plenty of radios. Holden pitched the radio into the flames of the burning truck, grabbed Rosie Shepherd into his arms. His own head swam with whatever it was, his lungs burning. He started to run, dizziness washing over him. He forced himself to keep going.

The smell.

Running.

Flames silhouetted their bodies against the wall as he looked back. A mushroom-shaped cloud was dissipating over the parking lot. Gray and green smoke was filtering down around them. Holden fell to his knees, Rosie unconscious in his arms. She'd gotten a stronger whiff of it faster, he realized. She was so much smaller, even though she was tall for a girl. Still . . . He realized he wasn't thinking right, got to his feet. Rosie was still in his arms, his gun was still in his fist. Everything had to be all right. He tried running, couldn't do that, then tried walking.

Patsy Alfredi and Pete Villalobos sat waiting in a police car. "Wanna see something funny, Rosie?" Holden laughed.

Then there was a series of progressively more deafening roars from the Aviteck building and David Holden felt cold and everything in front of his eyes was green and his knees buckled. . . .

CHAPTER 19

He sat up, threw up, but somebody shoved a kidney-shaped dish in front of his mouth and then he felt the cold disembodied feeling he'd just felt—how long ago?—in the parking lot and . . .

David Holden heard them talking and he opened his eyes. He tried to ask about Rosie but his throat burned. He couldn't see right, his vision blurred, but one of the voices was very familiar to him. "You can trust these people, David—they're Patriots." Holden squeezed his eyes shut and then opened them again. He tracked to the face belonging to the voice as the voice continued. "I know you want to know about Rosie. Well, she took a stronger dose than you, but she's going to be fine. She's already awake, but she hasn't said much, just been throwing up. The doctors here have checked your lungs for damage and both of you are going to recover completely." The voice belonged to Lem Parrish. Holden stared at him. A woman in a nurse's uniform hovered behind him. Black. Mid-twenties. Very pretty. A doctor, balding, fiftyish, leaned over the bed and shone a flashlight into Holden's eyes. Parrish kept talking. "Something really important has come up and the doctor here—you don't want to know his name or the nurse's name—this is a private clinic—the doctor says he'll release both of you by tonight. . . ."

"T—"

"Yeah, David. You and Rosie have been out of it for almost twelve hours. But if you take it easy for a

95

little bit, they can release both of you. You know, no running, no vigorous exercise for a day or so. But something really important."

"Rosie's . . ."

"She's fine, David." Lem Parrish smiled.

David Holden closed his eyes.

CHAPTER 20

Roger Costigan had expected someone would go to Chicago, had them followed, or simply had the airports serving Metro staked out. That was the only thing that made sense. It was impossible for Luther Steel to imagine that any of his own men—Runningdeer, Le-Fleur, Randy Blumenthal, or, certainly, Clark—would have betrayed them. And Director Cerillia had used a pay phone to call back to another pay phone, so a tap was out of the question unless the NSA was working for the bad guys, and that was just as impossible. The pilot, of course, was a potential leak, but he was not only Mr. Cerillia's pilot, he was also Mr. Cerillia's son-in-law, which narrowed the possibilities for deception still further.

Cerillia, an old hand in Chicago, had given Luther Steel a name, saying, "Trust this man with your life if you have to. I trusted him with mine. If he were to betray the United States, then we'd better all hang it up, because we've lost."

Luther Steel had checked the address twice, then again. It was correct unless somehow he'd miscopied it over the telephone.

Luther Steel knocked on the door. Bill Running-deer wearing his raincoat despite the heat in the empty, rather dirty-looking hallway was with him. Under the coat Runningdeer had the Uzi.

The hallway smelled of chitterlings and mildew. The building was one of the few standing on the block. But it was the West Side, and in some places the West Side of Chicago still bore the devastation of the self-destructive futility that followed in the wake of King's assassination.

The door opened six inches. There wasn't any chain, and the face visible through the crack looked old and worn. It was a black face, Steel expecting that from the location. "Yes?"

"I'm Rudolph Cerillia's . . ." What was he? Employee? "Employee" would sound stupid. Was it right to call himself Mr. Cerillia's friend?

"If you're Rudolph Cerillia, boy, I'm Charlton Heston." The old face laughed.

The last time someone had called him "boy," Luther Steel had told the speaker to fuck off, which of course had degenerated into a fistfight, which, upon reflection, Steel supposed he'd really wanted. But that had been almost twenty years ago when somebody had slammed a door in a black woman's face and he'd been a kid in college and the person calling him that had been a half-drunk biker with a southern drawl that someone could have cut with a dull knife. And the girl had been pretty and Steel had wanted to impress her.

In the nearly two decades intervening, Luther Steel had met more Southerners, learned that Southerners were basically just like everybody else and a growing number of them held doors open for black women instead of slamming them, and he'd learned that punching out a slow-moving drunk was no big trick and not worth the trouble. And the only girls he cared about impressing were named Steel, just like he was.

"I meant to say, sir, that I'm Luther Steel. I'm an associate of Rudolph Cerillia. He told me you'd expect us."

"Who's the Indian?"

Steel swallowed, glanced uncomfortably at Bill Runningdeer, then heard the old man on the other side of the door start to laugh. "I'm only kidding. Come on in, fellas." The door opened up and the right side of a tall, clearly once-athletic man somewhere in his late sixties came into view. Luther Steel wondered what the man held in his left hand.

"If you've got a gun, sir, it's only fair to—"

"Of course I've got a gun," the old man laughed, Steel turning around and seeing the weapon for the first time as he passed through the door. "You think I look like an idiot? Do I have a gun! Come on, guys." The gun looked like a submachine gun, was all black, and wasn't really pointed at either Steel or Running-deer. The hand holding it was long-fingered like a pianist's or surgeon's and looked like it could match a vice for foot-pounds of gripping force. Steel looked into the face more closely. The chocolate-colored black man's eyes were blue. It was a disarming appearance. "So, this is the FBI, huh? You're Rudy's best man?"

Steel almost started to say "I am?" but didn't.

The old man went on. "Rudy said to help you guys. So I guess I'll help out."

"Mr. Saddler—"

"Call me Rocky or don't call me at all, boy."

"My friends call me Luther."

"That's a hard name to swallow, Luther is." Rocky Saddler nodded grimly. "And the Indian here, he's William Runningdeer." It was a statement, not a question.

"Just call me Bill, sir." Runningdeer smiled.

"Well—Luther, Bill, and Rocky. Doesn't sound much like the new Three Stooges or a good name for some white law firm, but I guess it's gonna have to do. I gotta get my coat and some stuff. Grab a chair if you want." The apartment was spotless, but looked like something out of the sixties, right down to Beatles and Aretha Franklin records visible beside the stereo. "Just 'cause the building looks like some giant crapped on it doesn't mean this apartment isn't clean. Had a roach in here five years ago. The landlord brought it in in the cuff of his pants. Last time I ever let somebody come in with cuffs." And Rocky Saddler turned and disappeared through the open doorway behind him, the bedroom Steel presumed.

Steel looked at Runningdeer and shrugged.

Bill Runningdeer whispered hoarsely, "This guy's the fella Cerillia—"

"Whoa . . ." Steel said. On the wall, inside a handmade-looking glass display case, there was a Congressional Medal of Honor. Luther Steel walked toward the case.

He heard Rocky Saddler's voice behind him, kind of chuckling, Steel thought. "I like the looks of my Silver Star better, kind of more simple and elegant. But, hey—I'm glad to have it, even more glad to be alive to look at it."

"This is—" Steel started.

"Mine. Damn right. You don't believe me, after I help you get the goods on this damn child pornographer traitor bastard, you go ask Rudy who bailed out his ass and got one of those at the same time, huh?" And Rocky Saddler just smiled.

CHAPTER 21

"This is a TEC-9. This is a barrel extension. It's smooth-bored but makes it a damned sight easier to hold on to when you fire from the hip a lot. Each one of these magazines holds thirty-six rounds. I like 115-grain JHPs myself, 9mm of course. Federal's my first choice, but these days ammo's hard to come by. The sling makes it easy to carry around." Luther Steel just stared as the old man, Rocky Saddler, he corrected himself, threaded the barrel extension (which certainly looked like a silencer) onto the black firearm. "Looks like a subgun, but isn't, which before all these crazy emer-gency measures came through made it a lot easier to own legally. These days, nothing is. And since most submachine guns are only used in full auto for room sweeping, for most purposes this is just as good." He was attaching the sling now through two welded-on slots. The sling in place, Rocky Saddler put a full-length magazine up the gun's magazine well. "I don't rack the action until I'm expecting trouble," Saddler noted.

"Mr. Saddler—" Bill Runningdeer began.

"Rocky."

"Rocky. What if—"

"What if I'm not expecting trouble and trouble comes along anyway? 'This.'" From under his wind-breaker (Steel hadn't seen it and he usually prided himself on his ability to spot an armed condition) Rocky Saddler took a Browning High Power, the original single-action P-35. The bluing looked spotless in the light from the almost miraculously still-functioning streetlamp.

"I, ah—I see," Bill Runningdeer said slowly.

"Here's the way I figure it." Rocky Saddler nodded slowly, lighting a cigarette. Some older people looked odd smoking, Steel had always thought. But Saddler looked like some character in a sophisticated drawing-room comedy when he lit up, as if he owned the world. "Costigan's warehouse won't be the place he's got anything incriminating stashed, but maybe in the office inside he'll have left some clue which'll point us in the right direction. Don't worry about shooting anybody. The guys who work for him aren't regular security guards. They're street-gang people. I think they're FLNA. If I knew for sure, I'd have offed 'em a long time ago. So if they shoot at us, don't be worried about shooting back."

"Ah—" Luther Steel began.

"Now don't tell me you don't want to shoot anybody, Luther. I mean, I didn't assume you were a nutball. Nobody wants to shoot anybody unless there's a good reason for it. If we have to shoot, there'll be a good reason for it, so lighten up. If I've ever seen a prime candidate for ulcers, you're it. I'm seventy-three years old—"

"You're what?" Steel sputtered.

"Seventy-three. I joined up with the Army during World War II and stayed in for Korea. But, like I was saying, I'm an old guy, for God's sake. I don't have ulcers. That's 'cause I learned to lighten up, Luther. And you've gotta lighten up too. Take the advice of somebody who's been there and back at least six times and relax. If you look at this like kind of exciting and maybe potentially a little fun, then, hey"—Rocky Saddler grinned, gesturing expansively with his TEC-9 assault pistol—"life's a lot easier. Okay?"

"Yes, sir." Luther Steel just nodded. He guessed

they were going into a warehouse full of antiques to brace some street-gang people masquerading as security guards and probably going to get into a gunfight and, of course, that he should be careful to have a good time.

Rocky Saddler slapped a large adhesive bandage over the rental car's dome light to mask it, then stepped out onto the street.

Bill Runningdeer started to laugh, saying, "Clark Pietrowski'd love this old guy—hah!"

CHAPTER 22

Rose Shepherd didn't feel like driving, didn't feel like eating, but decided she could definitely use a drink even if it did make her start throwing up again. She couldn't remember the name of the chemical the doctor had said had zapped her, but she'd know it if she smelled it again, she thought. Probably a good long sniff of alcohol would put her away, but she was willing to risk it.

The car stopped, and David—who didn't look in such hot shape either but always looked cute to her anyway—helped her out. Lem Parrish was walking up to the front door of his house and Rose took David's arm. She was wearing one of Morgana Parrish's dresses. For that matter, she was wearing some of Morgana Parrish's underwear. Real silk. "Far out," she almost said out loud.

Lem and Morgana didn't have any children, which was maybe why Morgana could afford silk slips.

Morgana stood at the door, ushered them in, and smiled. "Hi, David. Rosie—you look terrific in that dress."

"It's a terrific dress," Rosie said, not knowing what else to say. It really was a terrific dress. White. Linen. Kind of blousey on top and the skirt so full somebody could have made curtains out of it. The shoes were a little tight, but at least they were open-toed and slings. She could cope.

Rose Shepherd realized everything was a little blurry, but she didn't really worry about it. The dress was loose enough on top that she had the little Model

60 in the Ken Null holster on under it, and the sweater over her shoulders covered the straps for the holster. And anyway, David would take care of her.

"Did you fit all your guns and knives into that purse too?" Morgana asked, ushering them through the living room, which looked like something out of a woman's magazine, and toward a couch that looked like something out of Buckingham Palace.

"Actually, just my .45, Morgana. The knife's strapped to my thigh. See?" And Rose Shepherd hitched up the left side of the dress and showed her.

Lem Parrish started to laugh. "Drinks anybody? Honey—when's dinner?"

"In about five, Lem," Morgana said over her shoulder with a toss of her wavy hair as she disappeared toward the kitchen.

"You know, Morgana's always been a terrific cook. I mean, her parents were rich and everything, but her mother—a really nice lady—always told her that it was fine to have maids and everything else but that when a man came home at night, he was entitled to a home-cooked meal made by his wife. I hope you guys like spaghetti."

Rose Shepherd almost laughed out loud. Any idiot could make spaghetti. You boiled water, tossed in the spaghetti, let it get a little cooked, got ready to drain it, and poured the spaghetti sauce out of the bottle into a saucepan—and wham! the cordon bleu strikes again!

"Make mine a beer, Lem. Way I feel, anything stronger'll put me under the table," David called across the room.

Lem asked, "What can I get for you, Rosie? Come on, be imaginative." She started to tell him a Singapore Sling but she didn't quite know what that was anyway. "How about a Black Russian?"

"How about a black FBI agent instead?" Rose Shepherd laughed. She didn't remember sitting down on the couch, but apparently she hadn't done it carefully so her dress was halfway up her thighs. She got things in order.

"No—it's not gonna be Luther Steel. It's Clark Pietrowski that's coming."

"Old Clark, huh? Hey. He's a good guy."

"I just met him a few hours ago, really. But he seems like a nice guy." Parrish nodded.

Should she be silly or conservative? "Give me a Salty Dog without the salt, okay?" She decided on conservative.

"Go light on the vodka with that, huh, Lem," David called across the room, holding her hand. With any other man she would have popped him one. But David usually knew best. "You feeling okay, Rosie?"

"Tired and a little woozy. The spaghetti'll make a new woman out of me," she reassured him. "I should go see if Morgana needs some help in the kitchen." She stood up, walked in the same direction Morgana had, and hoped for the best. She'd met Morgana Parrish three times before, the first time at a Patriot meeting at a pistol range before everything had sort of exploded. Morgana had been the only woman there with a Gucci bag and a diamond-studded ladies Rolex. But she seemed nice enough, Rose Shepherd told herself.

She found the kitchen. "Can I help, Morgana?"

"Would you like to toss the salad, Rosie? If you need one, there's an apron just inside the pantry."

"You bet." Rose nodded. She went to the pantry, the only apron there was one that looked like somebody would wear it for a garden party, but she figured she'd better go with it since the dress was borrowed. She ducked her head through the strap for the bib and tied the apronstrings in a bow at the small of her back as she started looking around for the salad. She found it. She started tossing it.

"I think it's just wonderful the way you live with

all those men and fight the FLNA, Rosie," Morgana told her.

She looked at Morgana, wondering how the salad would look all over Morgana's floral-print sundress. She decided that it wouldn't be noticed so abandoned the idea. "Well, gosh, somebody's gotta do it," Rose told her.

"But I mean, carrying a gun and everything and fighting like a man. I mean, how do you wash your hair?"

"With shampoo. It's the rinsing that's the tough part, Morgana."

"I'll bet," she agreed. "I mean, some women are so one-dimensional, you know? Do you like a lot of garlic on your garlic bread?"

Between looking at the salad and smelling the spaghetti sauce, she was about ready to barf. "No—not a lot of garlic, really. I want to keep my breath kissing-sweet or whatever they say."

"Ohh! I know what you mean. He's a hunk, isn't he?"

"David? Yeah. I guess he's a hunk."

"I mean, that dark, wavy hair and everything. It was just terrible about his wife and children."

She stabbed a tomato wedge. "Yeah. It was terrible."

"I think it's just the best thing that you and he have—well, you know."

"I know," Rosie told her. The salad was tossed. "Do you want this in the other room?"

"The dining-room table's all set. Why don't you put the salad on the table and get the fellas to sit down and I'll bring everything else in—okay?"

"You bet." She figured it was safe to ditch the apron. She hung it back in the pantry and took the salad and the cruets of oil and vinegar—she hated oil and vinegar—and started into the dining room.

She heard Clark Pietrowski's voice: ". . . evidence that Gamby's with the FLNA. But it looks too good to be true. And I'm still bettin' on Costigan as our boy. So I take a real hard look at the signature. I realized that if it wasn't Gamby, it was a pretty good job. But I can't trust going through regular channels, see." She set the salad on the dining-room table, walked back into the living room, and sat on the arm of the couch as she plowed through the borrowed purse. She found her cigarettes, offered one to David. He took one. She lit his, then hers. She saw a drink on a flower coaster on the coffee table and assumed it was hers. It looked like a Salty Dog. It tasted like one, but weak on the vodka. She noticed her borrowed sweater was on the couch and she didn't remember taking it off, threw it around her shoulders, closed her eyes tight for an instant. It was a good idea the drink was weak on the vodka. Clark was still talking: ". . . named Eddie Chelewski." She opened her eyes. She knew the name. Chelewski was a forger. And supposed to be a pretty good one at that.

"Chelewski," Clark went on, "tells me he knows who did it. But he figured I'd know too. And so suddenly, it dawned on me and I looked at everything in a whole different light. There was only one guy who could make a forgery so good that it could hope to pass the kind of handwriting analysis tests documents like those would have been given."

"What kinda stuff, Clark?" Rose asked. "I mean, maybe I missed something." She was inhaling the smoke hard. "Oh—everybody's supposed to come into the dining room and eat." She stubbed out her cigarette. David finished his beer. Clark took his drink and Lem took his. She took the Salty Dog, David at her elbow. David helped her with her chair, David and the rest of the men standing until Morgana sat.

"If it's all the same to everybody," Lem Parrish began, "let's bow our heads. David? Would you?"

David cleared his throat. "For that which we are about to receive, we are profoundly grateful, and grateful, too, for the good comrades with whom we share it—amen."

Morgana began passing things. Rose did too. David was like most men. He'd forget to pass and she had to elbow him twice.

"What were you guys talking about in there?" Morgana asked.

Clark Pietrowski looked at Lem Parrish and then at David, both men nodded almost imperceptibly. "Documents—a whole slew of stuff—that show Harris Gamby's with the FLNA, Mrs. Parrish. Like letters from him to this guy Johnson/Borsoi, who's supposed to be the head honcho around here. Jazz like that. Too good to be true. The kinda stuff we wanna get on Roger Costigan. I briefed Lem on that. So close to the kinda stuff we want, it hadda be faked."

"Roger Costigan?" Morgana repeated. "Don't forget the salad. Rosie tossed it."

"Roger Costigan's a traitor, it appears, Morgana," Lem Parrish said.

"Okay. So," Rosie asked Clark Pietrowski, "what'd the snitch forger say?"

"We both agreed," Clark began again through a mouthful of food. "Hadda be Charlie Lang."

The name didn't ring a bell. Rosie nibbled at her food. Clark kept talking, wiping his mouth with his napkin between bites. "Charlie was the very best ever. Until he slipped up and crossed some guys we were getting ready to indict. When they started singing to cop some leniency with the U.S. Attorney, one of the guys they mentioned was this Charlie Lang. He was forging everything from checks to bonds. But his real specialty was art forgeries, historical stuff, not paintings. Like letters signed by George Washington or Thomas Jefferson. Stuff like that. The forgeries were so good that nobody could tell they weren't genuine. Some of his stuff is probably still out there in the hands of private collectors who paid a fortune for what they thought was the genuine article lifted out of some museum collection or something.

"When they arrested Charlie Lang," Clark went on, "he sang his head off, cooperated every way possible except shining the U.S. Attorney's shoes or kissing his—his petutie. He did time in a minimum-security facility, rehabilitated. He's the vice-president and general manager for Cedar Ridge Islands now."

Rosie nearly choked, and David turned toward her solicitously, patting her gently on the back. Tears came to her eyes. "Cedar—"

"Cedar Ridge Islands, yep. Hangout for the rich and famous, luxury resort."

Morgana smiled and asked, "Why would a man with a fine position like that stoop to forgery again?"

"How'd he get the job in the first place?" David asked.

"Answer ya both," Clark told them. "He was in the slam with the owner of Cedar Ridge Islands, Lowell Bordeau. Bordeau was in for tax fraud. Bordeau hired him when they both got out. Bordeau died and his family kept Charlie Lang on because he was the only one who could run the place at a profit, which was why Lowell Bordeau was in for tax fraud to begin with. It's one of the biggest money-making resorts in the country nowadays. And why would Charlie Lang get involved with forgery again? Maybe he's into something he shouldn't be and he's bein' blackmailed into it or maybe he's an FLNA sympathizer or, just maybe, he's in it for some bucks. The interesting kicker is that Roger Costigan owns a condominium there right off the golf course on the main island. What if that little book you discovered, Professor, the one with all the stuff in it that looked like accounts or something but was written in code—what if that's got somethin' to do with Cedar Ridge Islands? You ever wonder where all these FLNA guys that aren't gangbangers come from? And how do they get into the country in the first place, huh?" Clark smiled, evidently pleased with himself.

Rose Shepherd put down her fork. If she ate another bite, her stomach would go one way or the other.

David said, "Identities, finances, the whole nine yards, even entry—it could all be accomplished right there."

"He knows me," Clark Pietrowski said. "I was involved in the bust that nailed him. Only a little bit, but if he remembered, we'd be screwed. I didn't talk to Luther on this yet; he's been so tied up. So I played it on my own. And this could work, Rosie, David, if you guys are game to try. I figure we need somebody inside and somebody outside if we're gonna get any action fast. And the election's only days off. So—one of you gets a job at Cedar Ridge Islands and the other goes down there as a guest—"

Rosie Shepherd interrupted him. "And the best kind of person for an inside surveillance is a black or a woman, right?"

Clark grinned. She wished she had her borrowed purse so she could light a cigarette. "And Luther isn't available," Clark told her. "Ever wait tables? I did some checking. They need waitresses."

She looked down at her borrowed linen designer dress. "In college, a little bit."

"Did you go to college?" Morgana asked, sounding sincerely shocked.

Rosie looked at her. "Police Science, honey."

CHAPTER 23

Rocky Saddler moved like a cat, and in his black clothes he almost looked like one. They crossed through a rain-slicked, garbage-scented alley, Steel's right fist tight on the butt of the P-226, Bill Runningdeer's right hand in the side pocket of his raincoat, the Uzi slung underneath the coat and the pocket slit through so all that was necessary was to throw open the coat and shoot.

Rocky Saddler stopped at the end of the alley. "There we go, boys." And he gestured with the Inter-dynamics assault pistol toward a shockingly modern one-story building that looked more like a modern church than a warehouse. "I did what checking I could. He's got an office in the back of the building. No safe. So he must keep whatever's valuable in his file cabinets, his desk, or in some secret compartment. Interesting rumors about some of the guys who work for him as security guards. But you can see for yourself." On that cryptic note and with a cautionary "Keep low! Move fast!" Saddler took off into the street, Luther Steel at his heels. It would have been possible to pass the old man but not easy, Steel realized. To be this fit at such an age was incredible.

Saddler, Steel, and Runningdeer, keeping to the shadows, reached the far side of the street, beside the warehouse wall. The wall was smooth, pressed red brick. There were windows, a little too high to see in and heavily grated. "Wired for an alarm system. But we've got that knocked," Rocky Saddler advised. "And by the way, all his security people carry subguns, fellas." Steel looked at Runningdeer and, as he did, reached under his sport coat for one of the twenty-round extension magazines for the Sig pistol. He swapped it with the fifteen-round magazine already in place and returned the standard-length magazine to the carrier. It was misting a little, and the K-Coated Sig had a fine film of moisture on it. He reminded himself to clean the P-226 if he got out of the warehouse alive.

Rocky Saddler ran along the perimeter of the building. Steel followed him and suddenly wondered if the old man had all his wits about him. What if his vigorous physical appearance belied a senile mind? But Rudolph Cerillia had said to trust Rocky Saddler. Steel shivered slightly even though it was a warm night. . . .

They were spending the night in the Parrishes' spare bedroom. David was cleaning their guns—he was the only person she would trust to touch her Detonics Servicemaster—and she was on the telephone. "Yeah, Eileen? This is Rosie—Rosie Shepherd?"

"Rosie! Kid—watcha doin'? I read about ya in the papers and the news and stuff," Eileen Fisher enthused.

Rose Shepherd smiled into the receiver. "Keepin' busy. Look—I need a favor, okay?"

"Name it, kid."

"Okay. I'm goin' undercover for the—the you-know-who, huh? So. I need a reference. You still the night manager at Kelly's?"

"Damn right. Kelly wouldn't know how to run a restaurant without me. Evening's when he gets all the payin' customers."

"I'm applying for a job tomorrow. Giving the name Roslyn Simmons. I'm gonna tell 'em I worked at Kelly's every night for the last six years. I want you to tell whoever calls to check that I'm the best waitress you ever had, you hated to see me go, the whole nine yards. I'm tellin' 'em I quit because I couldn't take working just nights, see? Tell 'em I worked for Amici's before I came to work for you. For two years. Worked there until it closed down, okay?"

"Sure. You're gonna hate bein' a waitress."

"I tried it in college. You're damn right. How's your worthless husband?"

Eileen Fisher laughed. "Just like a Klansman, honey—a wizard under a sheet."

Rose laughed. "Look—I gotta run. Thanks, Eileen."

"Be careful, kid—and hit your tables quick so the busboys don't rip ya on tips."

"I'll remember that. See ya. Bye."

"Best, kid."

Rose Shepherd hung up the telephone.

David looked over from the nightstand, where he was assembling her Detonics. "She going to cover for you?"

Rose Shepherd stood up, feeling a little sexy in the silk slip, a little stupid because she was still wearing the shoulder holster with her little Model 60 in it. "Yeah." She looked at the bed. She looked at David.

He racked the slide a few times, then put the magazine back up the well. "Let me wash my hands, huh?"

Rosie Shepherd shrugged out of the shoulder holster, sat down on the edge of the bed, and started rolling her stockings down. . . .

Like the most accomplished burglar—Luther Steel wondered just what Rocky Saddler had done for a living or still did—Rocky bridged the wires for the burglar alarm on the front door—"Nobody ever uses a front door, so nobody really watches it that well"— then worked a glass cutter with a small but evidently powerful suction cup, cut a hole in the door, and reached inside to turn the lock open.

Rocky Saddler walked into Costigan's antiques

warehouse, Luther Steel right behind him. Now Steel knew how David Holden had felt on the other Costigan job—like a common thief. Bill Runningdeer followed him in. Rocky closed the door, released the suction cup, and placed the circle of cut glass on the floor beside a potted plant. On closer examination the potted plant was a fabric phony. But it looked like a cactus, even from up close.

Rocky Saddler walked past the reception desk, pulled out a PCS set, selected the right lock pick, and went to work on the inside door. Steel looked at Runningdeer. Runningdeer shrugged, his right hand still inside his raincoat.

"Okay," Saddler whispered hoarsely, opening the door, passing through, Steel and Runningdeer following him. Saddler reached into the pocket of his windbreaker. "Don't remember terrain features as well as I used to." Steel peered over Saddler's right shoulder and saw a hand-drawn map of the interior of the warehouse.

"Where the hell you get that, Rocky?"

"Guy who polishes the floors once a week. Used to be a client."

"Client?"

"Didn't Rudy tell you boys anything? I'm a shamus, a private eye. Shit—let's stop talking and get going!" Rocky Saddler broke into a run along a narrow, wood-paneled corridor, executive offices or something on either side. At the end of the hall was a single wood-paneled door. Saddler stopped before it. "Another alarm, just like my buddy said. Just be a minute." And Saddler set to bridging it just like he had the alarm on the outside door.

A seventy-odd-year-old black PI with a Congressional Medal of Honor and a Silver Star to his credit? Steel shook his head, wanting to think he'd been injured on the airport tarmac and this was all a hallucination. Unfortunately, he realized, it wasn't.

"Got the sucker. Come on, boys," Saddler hissed, opening the door, slowly at first, then all the way.

Inside, beyond the door, it was dark. Saddler caught Steel's hand as Steel reached for his flashlight. "Eat more carrots. Won't need light. Follow me and stick close." Saddler moved swiftly ahead, Steel barely able to see his hand in front of his face, keeping almost on Saddler's heels so he wouldn't lose him, Steel's right palm sweating inside his glove as he gripped the Sig more tightly.

Saddler stopped, Steel almost crashing into him. "Hear that?"

"Hear what?"

"Shh!"

Saddler moved on, more slowly now, his TEC-9 a black silhouette against the deeper blackness of the warehouse and his clothes.

Steel heard something too. Voices, either very distant or whispering.

Runningdeer tapped Steel on the shoulder and Steel nodded to him. He heard the rustle of fabric as Runningdeer freed the submachine gun from the raincoat.

There was a light ahead.

Saddler was moving toward it like some calculating moth about to kamikaze a candle flame. Steel wanted to stop and ask Saddler why he was going toward the security guards—evidently the owners of the voices—rather than away from them.

They rounded the corner of a wall of packing crates, some of the crates enormous. But in the antique business things would perforce be of varying sizes, shapes.

The light was so much brighter here that Steel almost squinted against it.

Saddler almost slithered, he moved so slowly, with Steel at his heels.

The wall of packing crates ended, and Saddler peered around it. Steel felt Saddler's hot breath against his ear. "Cokeheads. This should be all the guards. We take 'em out now. Cover me and back my play."

Steel started to protest, but Saddler disappeared into the shadows.

Runningdeer was beside Steel.

Steel felt his pulse rate increasing. There were nine men. There were three Uzi submachine guns on the table they sat around snorting their lines, and some of the men at least were visibly armed.

And Steel, Runningdeer, and Saddler were breaking and entering. What was Saddler going to do? Make a citizen's arrest? Or kill them? Steel's blood ran cold at that. What kind of man—

"Freeze, fuckers!" There was the sound of a bolt being racked as Rocky Saddler stepped into the cone of light from the bare yellow bulb overhead. The TEC-9 was in his right fist, the Browning High Power appearing almost magically in his left. Two of the nine men started to go for the Uzis. Steel moved to back Saddler's play but Saddler was too quick. "Come on, asshole— haven't killed a doper since breakfast and I've got the urge."

"Holy shit! It's Rocky Saddler!" One of the cokeheads fell out of his chair, got to his knees, raised his hands, the other eight men following suit.

Steel looked at Bill Runningdeer. "Beats hell outta me," Runningdeer observed.

"All right, kiddies—let's one at a time start putting the rods on the table and maybe you'll live to talk about this. Move it!" Saddler's voice, with no hint of age or infirmity, sent shivers along Luther Steel's spine. He wondered if men were still made like this. Or had God broken the mold when He made Rocky Saddler?

CHAPTER 24

Rocky Saddler identified the desk as "Louis the XVI" while two of the captured cokeheads turned it upside down and a third started twisting on one of the legs.

"This stuff's irreplaceable," Steel objected.

"Good copies. Not even an FLNA bastard would mutilate the real thing," Saddler said, lighting a Camel without a filter.

"You smoke?"

"Five a day. It's already tomorrow, but this is only number four. Let a habit get control of you instead of you controlling it and you're a fool—like these boys." Rocky Saddler gestured with the TEC-9 toward the three cokeheads who were dismantling the desk and the six who were on their knees at the far corner of the room, hands clasped over their heads, the fear of God written all over their faces.

"These men know you. How?"

"Would you know Judgment Day if it happened to you?" Saddler answered.

Steel didn't know what to say. It was the mark of maturity, he supposed, to know you were outclassed. He knew he was outclassed and felt that James Bond, Dirty Harry, or John Shaft would have reacted similarly.

The legs were off the desk. They were hollow. From within the legs small plastic bags of white powder poured onto the warehouse floor. "Cocaine, boys," Rocky Saddler announced. "What if Costigan's a banker for the FLNA? Think about that one a little." And Rocky Saddler looked at his three helpers and the other

118

six. "Costigan's people keep any records around here? If I don't get an answer I like—"

"Missa Saddler—they's a coupla loose boards under the rug in the main office."

"Show me, little man."

"Yessuh!"

The young man—perhaps twenty—didn't move from his knees until Rocky Saddler said, "You can get up, but really slowly, right?"

"Yessuh!" And, really slowly, the young man got up from his knees. . . .

The office, like a small antique showroom, had a genuine oriental rug. Luther Steel had learned the difference from his wife, who had always wanted one, but they had never been able to afford anything but good fakes. The floorboards pried up very easily, the cooperative security guard getting them up with a switchblade knife of which Rocky Saddler promptly relieved him when the boards were raised.

There was an address book. Luther Steel recognized Costigan's own hand. It was a small book. The contents were in code. "Let me see that," Rocky Saddler said, taking it from Steel's hands. "Hell. We used codes like this in World War II. Give me a few minutes." And then he looked at his nine charges. "These men, Luther and Bill, are tough. Not as tough as me, but they'll want to impress me, which means you guys so much as twitch or sneeze or pee in your pants, they'll shoot you dead. Has everybody got that?"

There was a sincere chorus of "Yes, sir!"

CHAPTER 25

"Roslyn Simmons" got the job. Rose Shepherd figured Cedar Ridge Islands was desperate for waitresses. She'd shown up before nine in the morning, which meant taking the ferry ride at eight-fifteen and being on the dock waiting for it by seven. Between the waiting and the ferry ride—no cars were allowed on the four dry spots off the coast that formed Cedar Ridge Islands—her purse had been passed through a fluoroscope, her body through a metals detector. She spoke with a Mrs. Twitchell, who was in charge of restaurant and housekeeping staff and filled out an application, then waited with her hands in her lap for most of two hours. There were some old women's magazines that she'd already read and a newsmagazine with an article calling the Patriots modern-day vigilante fanatics.

"I can check these references." Mrs. Twitchell was tall, thin, almost mannishly broad-shouldered, and her silk suit looked like it came from Paris.

"I'd expect that you would, ma'am."

"It's minimum wage. Roslyn, is it? And whatever loose tips you get and a cut of the fifteen percent surcharge we add on to all the guest checks. If you do well, the cut increases."

"That's wonderful, ma'am."

"What's your dress size?"

"I'm a size ten most of the time."

"You're a size ten if you want a job. We supply the uniforms and there won't be time for you to have one taken in or altered. I'm critically short of people for the main dining room. I'll check these references, and if you lied, you're in deep trouble. Take this application to the receptionist, fill out the Social Security forms, go see Mrs. Robertson in Building Three. The receptionist will tell you how to get there."

"Yes, ma'am."

"You can start with the lunch shift."

"Thank you, ma'am."

"Then you'd better get moving, hadn't you?"

In Building Three, Rose Shepherd met Mrs. Robertson, a black lady of about sixty. "Size ten, right?"

"Usually."

"These run pretty good. Try this on."

Originally, Cedar Ridge Islands sought a turn-of-the-century British look. Those who served in the main dining room were to reflect that image. The waitresses' uniforms were designed to look like upstairs-parlor-maids attire, Mrs. Robertson had informed her while she tried on a uniform. An ankle-length black dress with a full skirt, little white collar and white cuffs, a white lace-trimmed cap that was to perch on the top of the head like a too-small bottle cap, and a matching white apron that almost covered the entire dress and nearly required the services of a structural engineer to get into.

Rose Shepherd looked at herself in the mirror. She was tempted to throw up. "You look pretty good," Mrs. Robertson told her.

"Thanks, ma'am."

"Mrs. Twitchell tell you about the uniform charges?"

"No."

"You get two uniforms, two caps, and four aprons. The cost for them is deducted from your wages at ten percent a week with a slight carrying charge. The aprons and caps have to be starched and we launder and starch them here. That's a charge of five dollars a week. That's also deducted from your wages. Take this marking pen"—she handed Rose one—"and mark the aprons and caps. I'll give you a number and show you where to mark them. You're responsible for dry-cleaning your uniforms yourself."

"Dry cleaning?"

"They don't wash well. Try on the other uniform."

"Yes, ma'am." She was ready to kill and, to fit in as Roslyn Simmons, was unarmed. . . .

David Holden stood at the ferry's rail, watching Cedar Ridge Islands gradually taking on more shape, more definition. Four islands forming a small chain, they lay a half hour's ride off the coast. In hurricane season, Holden mused, they wouldn't be the place to be for the "In" crowd. Although the ferry took a half hour, he gauged that a fast powerboat could make the run in under ten minutes.

"Hi." There was a husky, warm, feminine voice coming from behind him.

Holden turned around, involuntarily stroking the fake mustache Mimi Baker had supplied him with. The spirit gum itched his upper lip. "Hi, yourself!"

"Let's see," she began. "You must be Mr. Hemmings?" She was tall, pretty, blondhaired and blue-eyed, and expensively dressed, her nails perfect as she almost cuddled the clipboard against the front of her sundress, her cleavage pretty perfect too. She extended her right hand. "I'm Cindy Brown. I'm with the Recreation Department and it's my job to interview people like you and find out just what we at Cedar Ridge Islands can do to make your stay more enjoyable."

Holden released her hand, betting with himself that she got some interesting answers.

She started reading from her clipboard. "Mr. Dan Hemmings. Doesn't play golf—my goodness! Plays a little tennis. Likes to shoot trap and skeet but isn't very good at it." She batted her blues up from the clipboard. The sea air was cool and there was a breeze that did interesting things with her hair. "I'm afraid we voluntarily closed our trap and skeet ranges until the crisis is passed. But we can improve your tennis game. And there are the theaters, there's the beach—how about scuba diving?"

Holden thought what his instructors in the SEALs would have said when he answered, "I don't swim very well. Just splash around a little. And I really came here just to relax, soak up a little sun, unwind. I understand the food's great too."

"Then—yes it is your first time here! Oh! Lucky you! You'll just love it, I know." She patted his forearm and smiled.

"I hope so."

"If there's anything I can do to make your stay more enjoyable—I mean anything at all"—and she lowered her voice, looked at him hard for an instant— "well—call me." She gave him a Cedar Ridge Islands business card with her name on it and her extension, their fingers touching momentarily. "And you're not going to get away with just being lazy"—she smiled— "I'll look you up and see to that."

She flitted off.

Holden looked after her for a moment, then turned back to look over the rail. He started to smile. If Rosie Shepherd caught him with somebody like Cindy Brown, she'd kill him. Holden lit a cigarette and watched the water. There had been the customary weapons check of the luggage before getting on the ferry and the customary pass through the metals detector, but he was used to that.

It wasn't likely to be a weapons job anyway. If it degenerated to a fight, the purpose of the mission to Cedar Ridge Islands was lost and, in a pinch, he could try for a weapon out of the cache used by Cedar Ridge

Islands security. He and Rosie Shepherd were told all about that by Pietrowski. "They have all the licensing, all the paperwork, so it's all legal. Their security people are all deputized by the nearest offshore county. From what I was able to learn, they have handguns, obviously, but also riot shotguns, and submachine guns are available to their security people. The argument is that in this day and age the islands are very vulnerable to FLNA attack. And that makes good sense. Those islands could get hit anytime. And all those little coves on the main island would make it perfect for some bad guys to slip in without anybody spotting them. Charlie Lang takes personal charge of security from what I understand. Now he was never much of a gun man, but he's tough enough. So watch it."

Holden watched the whitecaps. He intended to watch his step too.

CHAPTER 26

David Holden showered and washed his hair, not bothering to replace the bandage on his right temple from the sudden encounter with the Plymouth Rock paperweight the night before last. He had a bruise and a rather wicked-looking cut but no stitches had been required and the cut was closed and forming a scab. He dressed in the clothes he'd acquired for the part of a well-off vacationer, the Rolex Sea-Dweller and his underpants the only things that were originally his. A pair of tennis-white slacks, overpriced white track shoes with socks that didn't come up over the ankle. A magenta short-sleeved knit shirt with a picture of a little animnal sewn in over the heart.

Using mousse given him by Mimi Baker, the waves that were naturally in his hair, and had been the bane of his existence when he was a boy when curly hair was considered sissy, were less pronounced. Mimi had also shown him how to comb his hair differently so he could give the effect of altering the shape of his face. The last thing he needed was for somebody to recognize his face from a post-office wall.

Underneath the knit shirt, instead of the flimsy elastic belt that was supposed to go with the slacks, he wore a sturdy brass-buckled Milt Sparks leather belt, the leather heavy although the belt was of conventional dress width. The belt was the closest thing he had to a weapon, although he'd known a guy in his service days—an Air Force sergeant—who was terrific at using a track shoe in a brawl. Holden had never picked up the technique.

It was nearly high noon and his luncheon reservation was for exactly twelve. Holden gathered up the overpriced wallet with the fake ID and credit cards, the handkerchief with the fake monogram, and his room key, and was off. With any luck Rosie would have gotten the waitressing job and he'd at least catch a glimpse of her.

Cedar Ridge Islands resort began around a single structure on the largest of the islands, the structure a house built at the turn of the century, very much the British hunting-lodge style: oak paneling and stone everywhere, with massive hearths and equally massive chandeliers. The main house, destroyed during a hurricane in the 1930s, had been used as the setting for a horror film set in the silent-film era and, because of the film, almost every room was recreated to be faithful to the period. The guest rooms, the dining rooms, the lobby, each room was based in whole or in part on the original. He read the brochure while waiting for the ten o'clock ferry.

Cedar Ridge Islands was something like an on-going costume party, but only the staff wore period attire. The women who serviced the registration and cashier desks were dressed like fine Victorian ladies, the bellmen like footmen, even horse-drawn carriages with appropriately liveried drivers and more footmen were employed to get the arriving and departing guests to and from the inn itself. The four islands were connected by causeways that could be crossed by foot, bike, or on horseback. The only vehicles as such were the golf carts on the far end of the main island, where Roger Costigan had his condominium. Likely nothing of great interest would be cached away there, but if he could get a look at the place it might be worthwhile.

He turned out of the flagstoned main hall (lobby) and into the main dining room. More elegantly dressed Victorian-looking ladies were in evidence, this time as hostesses, the waitresses in parlor-maid drag and the busboys in butler's aprons and striped pants. It looked like the perfect place for a Communist party convention, all the embarrassingly costumed workers waiting hand and foot on the wealthy.

One of the Victorian ladies showed him to his table. There was a blond harpist in Victorian attire playing. She smiled at him as he passed her. He wondered if Cindy Brown, the girl from the ferry, got into a Halloween costume as recreation director.

One of the second butler types poured water into a glass that looked like crystal. It couldn't really be crystal, Holden told himself. Holden looked at the menu. No prices were printed. He supposed it was one of those places where if one had to ask, one really couldn't afford it.

There was something that sounded like a turkey club sandwish but, instead of turkey, the "tender flesh of the finest Cornish hens" was substituted.

He heard a laugh and he looked up and nearly choked.

"You look stupid in that shirt."

"You look like 'Charlie's aunt from Brazil . . .' "

" 'Where all the nuts come from' and everything." Rosie grinned. "I feel like an idiot. Whatcha want? To eat, I mean."

He forgot what he wanted to order. A pianist began playing at the far end of the room, the harpist apparently on break. "Give me the club sandwich."

She smiled at him as she took the menu. "One BLT with a bird—right. Don't drink the coffee. It sucks."

"Iced tea?"

"All we got's unsweetened. Don't put too much sugar in it." She winked and floated away across the floor in her black dress, white apron, and cap. He just stared after her.

He drank enough iced tea to float out of the dining room. Each time Rosie came back to fill his glass she was able to exchange a word or two with him. She had passed by Charlie Lang's offices, not seen inside, however, but the locks looked easy enough to work, she figured. She'd try in the morning before Lang would be in his office. She had the breakfast shift and had to be on the 5:00 A.M. ferry over. He warned her to be careful, told her he'd seen nothing strange so far but was planning to check out as much of the resort on foot as he could throughout the afternoon and evening. Nothing strange except that everything was strange.

She brought him the bill. "If you leave me a tip, I'll break your arm," Rosie told him.

A sandwich and iced tea and a small dish of ice cream came to over twenty-nine dollars. He was glad the credit cards weren't in his name. He left a tip anyway, lest not doing so might look suspicious. . . .

Rose Shepherd stood at her station, making hot coffee and folding napkins. She watched David as he left the dining room. She wanted this to be over very quickly.

"Roslyn—table fourteen," another waitress told her.

"Thanks, Beverly," Rose answered.

The man and woman at table fourteen were drinking decaffeinated coffee so she took the pot with her, rustled her way between the tables—the noise from her clothing was driving her insane—and reached table fourteen. "Is there anything I can get you, sir?"

"I'd like some more coffee and so would my wife." Rose was proud of herself for anticipating that, poured the man's coffee first, then poured the woman's coffee, leaning past the little boy, whom she had already determined was brought to Cedar Ridge Islands simply because they couldn't find anybody stupid enough to keep him.

She felt something wet on her apron as her hand brushed against it. She looked at her apron. She looked at the little boy. He was lucky she had to stay in character or he would have had two broken ankles. "Didn't we like our ice cream?" Rose Shepherd inquired politely.

"Elmer! I told you never to do that again," the man snapped at the boy.

Elmer? No wonder the kid was rotten, Rose thought.

The woman said, "Don't shout at Elmer! It's only ice cream and you know what Elmer's therapist says about how it affects Elmer when you shout at him. I'm sure the girl has another apron. It's not as if he did it to one of the guests, for goodness sake!"

Elmer evidently liked to make soup of his ice cream, and when Rose poured coffee for Elmer's mother he poured the ice cream all over her from the waist down. The front of her apron was covered with it. Rose smiled her best Roslyn-the-waitress smile and told the woman, "It's no trouble at all, ma'am," then looked at Elmer, smiling with her lips but not with her eyes. "I hope you enjoy your stay here, young sir."

As she walked away Rose Shepherd heard the woman saying, "Isn't she a dear? They really know how to find good help here. I wonder if she's ever considered regular domestic work. She seemed to get along so well with Elmer!"

Rose Shepherd returned to her station, put down her coffee pot, fantasizing: "Someday he'll turn eighteen and try knockin' over a liquor store and—pow! The little sucker's mine!"

"Did you say something?" It was Beverly again, the girl she shared the station with.

"No—no." She started unwinding herself out of

the pinafore-like apron. "Give me a hand. Little brat at table fourteen—"

And Beverly started to laugh. "He got me yesterday!"

The lunch crowd was starting to thin out. Elmer and his parents left but left no tip. Rose started helping one of the busboys when one of the hostesses came over to her. "Roslyn."

"Yes, Mrs. Leer?"

"You and Beverly go to the kitchen and take the cart to Mr. Lang's office. Beverly will return here. You'll stay and serve. You're very fortunate to be asked to do this, so don't screw it up. Mr. Lang runs things around here and if he likes you, well, who knows?" She tossed her curls and smiled. Rose Shepherd just looked after her for a moment.

This was better luck than she could have prayed for. Luck like that didn't happen often.

Quickly, Rose Shepherd rustled her way back to her station, eyeing Mrs. Leer talking to Beverly, who was setting tables. The steak knives were the most peculiar-looking ones she'd ever seen, almost the size and shape of the old Green River-style knives used by the frontiersmen and mountain men in the days before the popularization of the Bowie knife. The tang, full width, ran two thirds the length of the wooden handle. She found the two sharpest ones she could in a hurry and dropped one inside the left-hand pocket of her apron behind her order book. The other one. What to do with that? The coffee maker's filters came in plastic bags and the bags were rubber-banded closed. She pulled off two rubber bands, looked behind her to be sure that no one was observing her, then unbuttoned and rolled up her right sleeve. She rubber-banded the knife inside her forearm, careful not to get the edge against anything that would bleed a lot, then tugged her sleeve down, closing the cuff. There were considerably better places for a woman to hide a knife, but there was no time to access any of them.

Beverly was already walking toward the kitchen. Rose looked into the polished stainless steel of the milk dispenser and saw herself well enough to verify that the stupid little cap was where it should be and her hair hadn't come down.

She started for the kitchen.

CHAPTER 27

Rocky Saddler told them the restaurant was famous all over the city of Chicago and all over the world. Luther Steel had protested that it wouldn't be a good place to discuss strategy. Rocky Saddler ignored that. The nine cokeheads from the warehouse were in the custody of six men from a local Baptist church who were all retired policemen or firemen, Rocky Saddler exacting a promise from them that they would mention nothing about himself, Steel, or Runningdeer or anything about cocaine unless they wanted to die first and be given over to the police afterward.

The restaurant, packed with truck drivers, business types, and police officers, was just noisy enough that Steel felt comfortable talking.

It was agreed that something further had to be done to nail Roger Costigan—and quickly.

The drugs would have been enough to sink Roger Costigan politically if there had been any direct evidence linking Roger Costigan to them. But it would be easy enough for him to blame a corrupt employee for using the Costigan antique business as a front for running cocaine. After all, Costigan didn't even work out of his Chicago offices. And then there was the sticky little matter of the cocaine being discovered illegally during a more grossly illegal black-bag job by federal officers working unofficially and without any sort of warrant, probable cause, or anything else.

"That book Rudy told me about," Rocky Saddler began, putting down the spoon with which he'd already ladled into himself two bowls of the most powerful chili Luther Steel had ever tasted. "That book and that little address book we found. Unless Costigan was just holding on to the porno book for some innocent reason, he's into stuff like that. So I called my granddaughter. She's coming over."

"Your granddaughter?" Runningdeer exclaimed, echoing Steel's thoughts.

Rocky Staddler grinned. "Relax—she's pregnant."

CHAPTER 28

"Hi! Mr. Hemmings!"

David Holden turned around, remembering his name just in time, slowing the bicycle, making a lazy figure-eight pattern with it, and stopping facing the direction from which he had come. Cindy Brown was peddling up toward him on a bicycle that evidently wasn't rented. It was the wrong color and looked somehow faster, sleeker.

She stopped her bike a yard from him and said, breathlessly, "You're in pretty good shape."

"How's that?"

"I checked at the bike barn. You were only five minutes ahead of me and this is a ten-speed." She patted the handlebars of her bicycle. "And I ride a lot."

Holden glanced at his Rolex. "Through for the day so early?"

"Afternoon off. I thought I'd look you up, and when somebody saw you going to the bike barn, well— here I am."

"On your afternoon off?" Holden smiled.

"I can always turn around."

"I like looking at you from this side, really. I was just, ah, taking a little tour of the islands. I wanted to see the condos too. I'm halfway thinking about buying one."

"The real estate people can help you," she told him earnestly.

"I'd, ah—rather look on my own, first. Real estate people always show you the good side of everything. Like with that little place I've got in the Bahamas," he

134

said offhandedly, hoping to bait the hook a little. "Could you show me? How about I buy you dinner tonight too? Or can't employees fraternize—"

"Only management level. I'm management level. Okay."

If Rosie worked the dinner shift, she'd want to kill him. But she'd understand. It was all in a good cause, because the more he thought about it, the more interested he was in Roger Costigan's condominium off the eighteenth green. . . .

Charlie Lang had to be in his late sixties. He was tall and thin and a little stoop-shouldered and had a sharp-featured face under his full head of gray hair. It looked as if he hot-combed it. Her eyes were drawn to his hands. They were the most beautifully manicured hands she'd ever seen in her life. She put the beef stroganoff before him and he looked at her. "Well?"

Beverly left after helping with the cart and she was alone in the room with him. The room was an office, exquisitely detailed, with the richest-looking paneling she'd ever seen, little mementos everywhere, autographed photographs of every celebrity she'd ever heard of almost littering the wall over the main fireplace. The floor was real stone, or a good fake, and animal-skin rugs—mostly bears—were everywhere.

She realized he wanted her to empty the stroganoff onto his plate. Rose Shepherd took two linen napkins and started to try her best.

"You're a little slow, girl."

Slow, my ass, she thought. "I'm sorry, sir, I'm new." She smiled.

"You're pretty, though. How'd you like to serve me every day?"

She didn't know what to say to that one. "I'd really be honored, Mr. Lang."

"I bet you would, girlie."

She hated men who called grown women that. "I really would, Mr. Lang" seemed like the right thing to say.

He told her, "Unfold my napkin; put it on my lap."

"Yes, sir." She swallowed. She took the napkin, shook it loose, had to reach halfway under the table to put it on his lap. "Is there anything else, sir?"

"You could unfold my napkin if I had one."

Rose Shepherd wheeled toward the origin of the voice, the inner office door. It was the man from the truck stop whom she'd shot in the arm, Johnson, his real name Borsoi. In his right hand was a Glock 17 9mm pistol.

Rose Shepherd reached to her apron pocket, the steak knife coming into her hand, moving it toward Charlie Lang's throat. She stopped cold. Charlie Lang had a revolver, just like her own little Model 60 .38 Special that she'd left in the trunk of the car back on the mainland. The gun was touching her right breast, and the look in Charlie Lang's eyes said he'd use it.

Borsoi/Johnson spoke. "I never realized you had such considerable domestic talents, Detective Shepherd. After I realized it was you who had shot me, I memorized your face. I saw your face in the restaurant. Now—where's David Holden? With his little band of Merry Men in Metro?"

Rose Shepherd almost said aloud "Thank God." But she didn't. He hadn't seen David.

"Drop the knife, Detective Shepherd. But be careful not to drop it on Charlie Lang or he'll blow off your tit and that would be a terrible waste."

Rose Shepherd dropped the steak knife onto the table. She looked at Charlie Lang, saying, "Next time I serve you, it's gonna be ten miles of bad road and a pile of shit."

CHAPTER 29

Rocky Saddler's pregnant—very pregnant—granddaughter, Marissa Steinberg, leaned over her grandfather, gave him a big kiss on the left cheek, then sat down.

Luther Steel took his seat, as did Bill Runningdeer. Marissa Steinberg looked no more than twenty or so, her hair Whoopi Goldberg-esque, and her skin was the color of cafe au lait. The effect was very pretty indeed, Steel thought. And she had her grandfather's blue eyes. "You're probably wonderin' why the last name of Steinberg. Right?"

Luther Steel didn't know what to say, but he was wondering.

"My husband's got an interesting background for a Moslem."

"Muslim?"

"No—he's from Egypt. It's a long story." She was digging into her purse, pulling out little books with pink- and blue-colored bindings and putting them down on the table between herself and her grandfather. The waitress came over, and before she could ask a question Marissa Steinberg said, "Coffee, honey—black like me." Rocky was evidently enjoying his granddaughter and was smiling a lot. Steel reflected it was either that or something in the chili. "So—I got all my books and all the ones my girlfriend Celine had. These are all Judeo-Christian names, but I figured that was okay."

"Right on, darling." Rocky nodded.

"So—let me see it."

"What?" Luther Steel said, feeling as though Rod Serling should appear at any moment in a 1960s narrow-lapel suit.

"The little address book, for criminy." She smiled, opening a cigarette case. But there were carrot sticks inside and she started chewing on one. "Like a carrot?"

"No, thank you," Runningdeer said. Steel took one and nibbled on it, still tasting the chili and crackers. "What?"

The little address book taken from under the floorboards in Roger Costigan's warehouse office was in Steel's right-hand breast pocket. He took it out, weighed it in his hand for a moment, then handed it to her.

She began leafing through it immediately. "This is a pretty simple code, Gramps," she told Rocky Saddler.

The carrot stick tasted like ordinary carrot.

"This guy Costigan is no genius. Look." She rolled the first page of the address book into a cylinder, adjusted its size from larger to smaller. "Bingo!"

Rocky Saddler looked over her shoulder. "That's my girl. So what do the numbers mean? Just a simple alphabetical code?"

"You got it, I bet." She opened one of the little books. It had a title that had to do with naming baby boys. "Okay. These numbers. Big deal. He's running them backwards, I bet. Look. Not all that many boys' names have eight letters." She flipped through one of the baby-name books. "Let's try Lawrence." She rolled the address book sheet again. "Nope. Ah—Reginald!" Steel looked toward the door, wondering if her husband had just walked in. But she was trying another boy's name. "This is it, Gramps. Get how it works?"

"Yeah, kid. Easy now."

"Look—I can't wait for the coffee. I'm late for class." She stood up before Steel and Runningdeer could, planted a quick kiss on Rocky's cheek—the right one this time—then said, "Nice meeting you fellas, huh? Pay for my coffee, Gramps. And drop those little books off at the apartment? Love ya!"

And she was gone.

Bill Runningdeer asked, "Is she a student?"

"No—she teaches ancient languages at the University of Chicago. Trying to make it through the summer quarter before she delivers."

"Oh." Luther Steel just nodded.

Rocky Saddler was decoding the notebook on the back of a napkin.

CHAPTER 30

Holden looked out across the water beyond the golf course, waves crashing over the beach that formed its perimeter. The sun was setting in the west, he mused, then laughed at himself. Obviously it was setting in the west, just where it should be. He needed a rest, not a trip to a posh FLNA staging area. And he needed Rosie Shepherd beside him, not the giggly effervescence of Cindy Brown.

Everything was perfect about her, the cocoa brown of her tan contrasted against the yellow of her shorts set, even the way the wind mussed her hair in an orderly fashion, just making her hair look prettier rather than disarrayed. "Which one is Roger Costigan's place?"

Cindy Brown looked up at him. She still straddled her ten-speed, Holden's bike leaning against a tree. "Roger Costigan?"

"The guy who's running for mayor of Metro. You know."

"It's that one," she said after a second, pointing to the unit right off the edge of the golf course. "It's that one over there."

"Must be a lot of famous people who come here," David Holden said, just to be saying something.

"You're Professor David Holden, aren't you?"

Holden reached for her, his right hand closing over her left wrist as he looked from side to side. No one sprang out at him from the bushes, no guns were pointed at him. He could always make a run for it into the surf. He was a strong swimmer, always had been.

"Aren't you?"

It was almost as if she were pleading for him to be David Holden. Holden released her wrist and smiled. "That's a silly thing to say. I thought you—"

"You are! After I met you again on the ferry I went back to the office and went through some old magazines. I never forget a face and, like you said, so many famous people come here, sometimes not using their right names, simply to get away. So I always notice faces. And I saw your face in one of the newsmagazines and it made me remember. I studied art." She smiled, her eyes softening with it. "I was pretty good. I ran the photograph from the magazine through the Xerox machine. Then I changed the hair and added the mustache."

Involuntarily, Holden touched at it. "You seem awfully eager for that reward they're offering for Holden. Dead or alive, isn't it? I've been told we look alike. That's why I grew the mustache. Sorry to disappoint you."

"You are David Holden. And if you aren't, I'm about to make a really big fool out of myself. Because I've been praying to meet someone from the Patriots, and if you aren't Professor Holden, I'm not only going to lose my job but maybe get us both killed."

Holden lit a cigarette. He carried his own, with Rosie's purse not available. "Look, Miss Brown— Cindy—look, ah—" Holden started to walk back toward his bicycle.

"Men come to Cedar Ridge Islands. Men with foreign-looking suits that don't fit them that well sometimes. The helicopter goes out to sea empty late at night and returns before dawn with men aboard. Mr. Lang always meets the helicopter and for the next few days you see the same men, but with better-fitting clothes. They ride the ferry back to the mainland, but they never come back to the islands. I think they're spies, maybe some of the people who are involved with the Front for the Liberation of North America. Because I read that some of the people are suspected of being foreign nationals, terrorists maybe. I think they come in by submarine or something and the helicopter flies out to sea and picks them up and brings them back in. That makes sense, doesn't it? I would have called the FBI or somebody, but I was afraid."

Holden's fists gripped to the handlebars of his bicycle. "Then why would you tell a wanted man like David Holden about it?"

"Who do you trust these days? But at least—do you remember the name Julie Dzikowski?"

Holden looked down at his hands. He kept saying the name to himself. There was something familiar about it.

"Didn't you teach a class at Thomas Jefferson University on origins of American government or something like that?"

"Julie Dzikowski," Holden said aloud, the name starting to take a face, hazy but there.

"I studied art at Thomas Jefferson. Julie was my friend. She was one of your students. She became a high school history teacher. She was killed on the same day your family was killed, but she was miles away." Holden shivered. "She always talked about you, about how nice a guy you seemed to be. Julie asked you once if her friend could come and sit in on one of your classes. Remember?"

David Holden let go of the handlebars and the sudden release of tension against it made the bicycle overturn. He didn't try to pick it up. "Theories on the Origin of American Government. Julie Dzikowski took two other classes from me. Dead?"

"There was a bomb that went off in the high school where she was teaching. I figured, well, if you were leading the Patriots, at least I could trust them. Please! Be Professor Holden!"

"You can't rip these things off that easily," he said, gesturing to the mustache. "Unless you use this chemical, you pull some of your skin off with it."

Cindy Brown came into his arms, and David Holden just held her for a moment.

CHAPTER 31

The first name decoded to Reginald Hastings. The second name decoded to William Bledsoe. The third name decoded to Thomas Krupov. The fourth name decoded to Harry Lawrence. There were thirteen names in all, and Bill Runningdeer said, "Hope it's an unlucky number for Costigan."

Rocky Saddler spent an hour on the telephone, then they left the chili place and drove to the far South Side, almost into Indiana.

They were at a closed steel factory. Rocky Saddler clambered over the chain link fence like a boy of thirteen and Luther Steel and Bill Runningdeer went after him.

The steel factory, its furnaces cooled, its smoke-stacks merely upthrusting cylinders, was like a futuristic ghost town, Luther Steel thought. And, like a ghost town, there was a "main street" along which they walked, the three of them abreast. All that was missing was Frankie Lane singing about a gunfight, Steel thought.

At the end of the street Rocky Saddler stopped, leaned against a low fence rail, and lit a cigarette. "We've got to wait awhile."

That turned into an hour. Steel became jumpy, and Bill Runningdeer's right fist never left the Uzi under his raincoat.

At the middle of the second hour a uniformed Chicago policeman, about thirty years old, started walking down the street toward them. He was black, about six feet tall, and his shoes gleamed in the lowering sun.

Steel looked at Rocky Saddler. "What's going on?"

"Trust him," Saddler said quietly. Holden saw Runningdeer's right shoulder tense beneath his raincoat. "Relax, Indian." Saddler laughed.

The Chicago policeman stopped a few feet away from them. There was a service revolver on his right hip in a standard presentation and a snub-nosed revolver in a cross-draw holster at his left side. Steel wondered what was under the department-issue leather jacket when it was cold enough to wear it.

"Reginald Hastings, Bledsoe, Krupov, and Harry Lawrence. William Bledsoe and Thomas Krupov sell pornography, the expensive kind, rare stuff imported from Europe and Asia, and they have a real discriminating clientele, some of their people real influential," the cop said in a rich baritone. "Reginald Hastings and Harry Lawrence cater to prominent male homosexuals. Lawrence has been arrested twice for contributing to the delinquency of minors. Hastings was brought up on second-degree murder charges in connection with a drowning death two years ago. The boy who died, his body showed evidence of considerable sexual abuse and there was soap in his lungs, like somebody'd drowned him in a bathtub. The charges were dropped for insufficient evidence. Here's a list of addresses." He took a few paces forward and handed a folded sheet of paper to Rocky Saddler. "Hastings would be your best bet, Rocky. You can get what you need out of him, but it would never stand up in court. There's a potential tie-in with that other thing, the cocaine, because Hastings is a user. He got so shook during that murder trial, he went on the stuff. Maybe he supplied your man and your man supplies him, huh?" The cop grinned, looked directly at Steel for the first time, then at Runningdeer. "Have a nice day. And watch out for

Hastings's place. He's got some mean-assed body guards." He made a little salute. "Sorry I was late. Got stuck riding herd on an accident for a while. The Dan Ryan's still backed up with a gapers' block if you're heading downtown. Take the Drive to Congress and the Kennedy and out and you'll be cool this time of day."

He turned around and walked off, Rocky Saddler calling after him, "Owe you one, my friend."

"Shit—I could help you a dozen times," the cop said over his shoulder, his voice trailing off as he walked, "maybe a thousand times and we'd never be even."

Rocky Saddler looked at Steel and at Runningdeer. "Wait until my pal's gone, then we gamble on Hastings. If we can get Hastings to agree to talk, you guys can blackmail Costigan out of the race."

"Tomorrow isn't that far off," Runningdeer mused aloud. "And the election's the next day."

"There's still time," Steel whispered.

There had to be.

CHAPTER 32

Rosie Shepherd was not on duty in the dining room, which was a mixed blessing as Holden was eating dinner with Cindy. There seemed to be plenty of waitresses, anyway, he told himself; that was probably the logical explanation for her absence, maybe a shift change or something. But she had to take the ferry over the next morning at five. If she'd left the islands already, or even if she hadn't, waiting for her tonight would be pointless, might attract attention. Just to be on the safe side, however, he would be up, down at the ferry docks to see her return to the islands from a discreet distance the next morning. He would probably never get to sleep with all he had planned. And the more he thought about Rosie, the more Holden worried. So he tried forcing her out of his mind. It had little effect.

He finished with his dinner, eating little of it, despite the excellent way in which it had been prepared and served. Cindy also picked at her food. They left, tickets reserved for them for one of the many plays that amateur and college dramatic societies put on throughout the summer on the islands. Cindy Brown, accompanying him, had assured him that Charlie Lang would be in attendance since it was opening night. And he wanted to see Lang, perhaps strike up a casual conversation with him. What good it would do, he didn't know. And then afterward, explore the wing of the inn where the oddly dressed visitors who arrived by helicopter before dawn were customarily billeted. And then wait up through the night for the chopper's

147

mysterious round trip, empty when it left, filled when it returned. If the chopper left at all. Cindy Brown said it was long overdue for another trip. He hoped she was right.

The play was Thornton Wilder's *Our Town*, an overly ambitious undertaking for most amateur theater groups (the Stage Manager still had acne) and always Holden's least favorite play because it was so terribly depressing. The production didn't disappoint him, both depressing and poorly done. Charlie Lang was not there.

A half hour into the production Cindy Brown whispered to him, "I can't understand it. Can you? I mean, he's always here."

"Let's go look for that helicopter," Holden told her, taking his little Mini-Mag Lite from beneath his blazer, adjusting the beam to pencil width, helping her from her chair in the darkened auditorium. "If anybody says anything about why we're leaving, say you took ill. It'll save your reputation and attract less attention."

When they left the theater the night was sultry. He took off his jacket, helping Cindy Brown into her shawl. It was one of those things that was more holes than yarn and he could never understand why women thought they were warm. He was hot, she was cold; he told himself there was no logic to it so why bother trying to understand it.

Horse-drawn carriages waited outside the theater and Holden helped Cindy Brown board one. "The inn, sir?"

"Only halfway. We'll walk the rest of the way," Holden said, easing down beside Cindy Brown.

"Right, sir." The driver brushed his whip against the gray draft horse's back and the carriage began moving. He could have run faster.

About a minute into the ride Holden made a point

of asking in a loud voice, "Are you feeling any better, Cindy?"

She looked up at him and winked. "Oh, a little. But I think you're right. A walk should perk me up."

It was a clear night, stars twinkling everywhere above them—a perfect night for aviation.

The road back toward the inn went along the sea, the golf course inland from them much of the time, the condominiums—those that were lit—twinkling richly in the distance.

The carriage approached a rise and Holden said, "At the top of the rise would be good, driver."

"Right, sir."

The carriage stopped at the top of the low hill and Holden stepped out, helping Cindy Brown down. She wore a pink sundress and sandals with no stockings and had a gorgeous tan, a richness to her skin under the light of the half-moon. As she stepped down she pressed against him. Their eyes met. Holden smiled, reaching out a few singles from his pocket and passing them up to the driver. Carriage service was part of the guest-service cover charge, but it would have been tacky not to tip.

"Thank you, sir. Have a pleasant evening. Hope you feel better, Miss Brown."

"Thanks," she called after the driver as he started the horse down the road. They waited, standing beside one another until the carriage was around the bend and out of sight. "The helicopter pad is about a quarter of a mile that way."

"I can go by myself if you'd like."

"These sandals are good walking shoes. Don't worry." And they started across the golf course to-gether. . . .

She had to go to the bathroom and refused to just let it happen. She kept working her hands on the cord that bound her wrists. Nothing. Her fingers were too numb to reach the second steak knife, the one rubberbanded up the right sleeve of her dress, and even if her fingers hadn't been stiff, the way she was tied she couldn't have reached it.

Rose Shepherd was tired, slightly sick to her stomach, and frightened—and embarrased.

They'd gotten her so easily.

When she'd pulled the steak knife out of her apron pocket, she had done it knowing that Johnson/Borsoi had the drop on her. And anyway, no purpose would have been served in raking the knife across Charlie Lang's throat. But the chance she had hoped for to use the second knife to parlay herself into a gun or just to escape never materialized. Once she dropped the knife, two other men entered the room, making it four to one, two submachine guns and two pistols against a steak knife up her sleeve.

There had been more questions about David, the threat of a beating, which hadn't happened yet—at least—then a walk. A long one. Through a side office and into a corridor behind it. No paneling here, just unfinished plasterboard and studs and rock. A walk along this corridor, moving downward it seemed, entering a basement from the side, then crossing the basement to a door. The door was opened and she was forced down the stairs, into a subbasement of some type.

It looked like the basement of a department store, except for the small photographic setup and the small printing press. But everywhere else there were racks of men's clothing, suits, and sport coats, shirts and even hats, and there were shoes in boxes on large carts. They took her past a room that was padlocked and there was a sign out front of it reading "No Smoking" in several languages, some of which didn't even use the same alphabet.

Then into this small room where she was now. A straight-backed chair was brought in, the kind used in the dining room, but the padded seat had a big stain on it. Maybe little Elmer had been at work again. They'd put her in the chair, Johnson/Borsoi keeping his pistol against the tip of her nose while they tied her up. One of the men with the submachine guns pushed away her skirts and tied her ankles together, then tied her ankles to one of the chair legs. Then her arms were forced around the back of the chair and her wrists were bound together. A length of the rope—it was the kind water-skiers use—was lashed over her thighs and tied beneath the chair, another around her abdomen and then tied tight. The ropes forced her into an unnaturally upright position, and aside from the fact that she had to urinate, her back was killing her.

Johnson said, "The subbasement is soundproofed. There's no reason to gag you, but it might make your brief stay with us a little more uncomfortable. Do you like helicopter rides? The spray of the sea?" And he'd stuffed a dinner napkin into her mouth as she started to scream at him, and then tied the napkin in place with another napkin.

He'd looked at his watch, saying, "See you at midnight, Detective Shepherd."

What time was it now? A helicopter? The sea? Despite herself, cursing herself for showing weakness, she was crying.

CHAPTERS **33**

The helicopter looked as though it could accommodate six or eight passengers and a crew. Holden remembered it being mentioned from the brochure. For condominium owners, the helicopter was available to fly them back and forth between the islands and the mainland so they wouldn't have to wait for ferry runs.

It was only a little after ten, and according to Cindy Brown, the chopper never left before eleven-thirty, most times closer to midnight.

With Cindy beside him, Holden made his way back to the executive-staff bungalows, mini-versions of the condos by the golf course but much closer together. She invited him in, but he told her he'd see her later, leaving her there and taking a back route she had described toward the north wing of the inn after he had asked her, "Where could I find some hand tools? You know, like a hammer, a screwdriver, like that?"

The north wing of the inn was where the men who returned with the helicopter customarily stayed.

The inn had several guest plans and the second floor of the north wing was one of the areas to which admittance was only gained by a credit-cardlike magnetic key. There was a complimentary bar there for the guests of that wing, Cindy told him. He wondered what else there was. He'd made a stop at the maintenance headquarters, a simple matter of scaling an eight-foot chain link fence with no wire at the top, using a rock to punch a hole through a side window in the tool barn, then, with his flashlight, helping himself to what he needed. Then back over the fence.

David Holden tried the trellis. It gave under his weight but only a little. No key for the restricted second floor of the north wing available. Rather than a door he would opt for a window. The old sack he'd found to carry the stolen tools in was strapped to his trouser belt.

By using the trellis and the first-floor balcony railing, he reached the base of one of the second-floor balconies, clambering over the railing. The rooms beyond the balcony were lit. He hid beside the sliding glass door, found a crack in the curtain, and, despite feeling like some sort of voyeur, peered inside. Lights on, a television playing. Nobody in evidence.

Holden crossed the balcony, went over the rail, jumped the four feet to the next balcony, and climbed on. Again, lights lit, the television on. The same channel as the first set. All the televisions in the building, apparently, when turned on automatically went to the preview channel for the pay-per-view cable movies. Both televisions he had seen from the balcony were on that channel.

Holden tried the third balcony.

The same story. Lights, television, but no people.

Holden consulted his tool bag, taking a small but hopefully adequate crowbar from inside and putting it to the lock for the sliding glass door. If he had known what he was doing, he realized, it would have been faster and easier to jimmy the lock, but he blamed his parents. He'd been raised in a decent neighborhood and taught that it was wrong to break into houses and steal.

At last the sliding door moved.

Holden caught up his tool bag with his left hand, the crowbar in his right as a weapon. With his right elbow he pushed open the door, then stepped inside.

There was a bedroom, a small sitting room, and a full bath. He checked the sitting room and bathroom, and although he found no one, he discerned several items of interest. There was a bottle of shampoo, a bottle of conditioner, a bottle of after-shave, an aerosol can of shaving cream, a razor, and a packet of blades. None of the containers was opened. A can of deodorant. The same, unopened.

In the sitting room there was a single bottle of generic whiskey, unopened, along with a single bottle of red wine, also unopened.

He checked the bedroom closet. A single large suitcase, a small attaché case, and a suit bag. Nothing in any of the cases except for a notebook (in which nothing was written), which was in the attaché along with two Bic pens and a cheap automatic pencil.

Holden left the room through the balcony doors, taking his tools with him. He jumped to the next balcony. Again, the same television program, previews for pay-per-view movies. It was quicker this time to jimmy the lock on the sliding glass door. He entered the room, quickly checked that there were no occupants, then inspected the bathroom. The assortment of personal hygiene products, the same unopened condition. No generic whiskey or red wine in the sitting room, simply bottles of soda pop. For a nondrinker?

The closet held an identical attaché case with an identical unused notebook, two more Bics, and an automatic pencil, even the same color as the ones in the other room. A suitcase of a different color and an identical suit bag. Apparently, Charlie Lang went for volume discounts.

Holden left and crossed over to the next balcony, checking his watch. Time for one more room. The third door jimmied so easily, he decided he might have a future in crime after all. The bathroom held the same products, the closet held an identical attaché with identical contents, a suitcase of a still different color, and an identical suit bag. This room's future occupant was evidently more specific with his tastes. A bottle of brand-name dark rum and a six-pack of Coke were in the sitting room.

Holden exited into the hallway. Under the crack in each of the doorways, he could see light. When he pressed his ear and a borrowed tumbler to the door, he could hear the same television station playing.

He reached the near end of the north wing, entered the bar. Exactly the same brands or generics as he had seen in the rooms were in the bar.

Holden slipped his tools under the sofa and let himself out.

It was almost eleven-fifteen. . . .

The urge to urinate had passed. The pain in her back had increased and she had no feeling in her fingers or feet. Rose Shepherd prayed that midnight would come, if for nothing else than to get her out of the chair. And there was no help for her. David might have missed seeing her waiting tables at dinner, but he wouldn't go looking for her, probably wouldn't notice she was gone until breakfast tomorrow. And by then . . .

She had been feeling nauseous for a long while, but she fought it. If she vomited with her mouth gagged, she'd only choke to death. She closed her eyes, no more tears left.

CHAPTER 34

Reginald Hastings's home was a mansion in the far northern suburbs. "Guy who lives at the other end of the block is a banker," Rocky Saddler interjected, as if reading Steel's thoughts. "I did a little job for him nineteen months ago."

"Nineteen? Not a year and a half?" Runningdeer asked.

"In my business, you've got to be precise," Saddler answered offhandedly.

The rented car was parked across the street from the entrance of the long driveway leading to the house. Luther Steel imagined it was only a matter of time until one of the suburban cops or a private security patrol drove by and started paying them some unwanted attention. There was no sign of the devastation of Metro here, although Chicago proper looked in parts like a war zone. But here, where the rich could afford all the security and high-visibility lighting that money and influence could buy, it seemed as if the FLNA didn't exist.

"There are three ways to get in," Rocky Saddler began, sitting beside Steel, who was at the wheel. "Crash through the gates, which with this car wouldn't be practical and would mean I'd have to disarm the fuel-line cutout that kicks in at impacts over fifteen miles per hour." Steel just looked at the man, amazed. "Second, we go over the fence and knock out the Dobermans. I don't like killing dogs. It isn't their fault some clown like this Reginald Hastings is using them to hide behind. And it's slow anyway. Third route seems the best. We drive up to the gate, get a security man down there, and shoot our way in. Any problems with that?"

"A lot, yeah—but if we've got to."

"We've got to, Luther. It's almost tomorrow. That gives you thirty-one hours if the polls open at six A.M. in Metro, right?"

Luther Steel couldn't argue with logic like that. "Let's do it."

Steel fired the ignition, the air-conditioning mercifully coming on. "Turn right into the driveway and hit the front gate, but not so hard you rack up the car, Luther. Then, Bill, you climb out and hit the gate button. You look white, so they'll be less inclined to call the police."

"Right, Rocky."

"We were doing a three-point turn and the accelerator stuck and we need to call the motor club or something—and don't let somebody call for you. Tell them you've got free towing but you have to call yourself so you can give the number off your membership card. Got that, Bill? And don't forget to offer to pay for fixing any damage to the gate."

"Right, Rocky."

"Okay, Luther—nice and easy." And Rocky Saddler slid down out of the seat and onto the floor below the level of the dashboard.

Steel blinked his eyes, then rammed the front end of the rental car into the gates.

No alarm sounded, unless it was silent.

Red lights came on all over the dashboard and Steel killed the ignition.

Bill Runningdeer stepped out, made a show of staring at the damaged car and damaged gate.

Runningdeer pushed the button on the communications panel beside the gate. "Hello in the house?"

After less than a second a voice came back: "You hit the front gate!"

"Look relax, huh? I'm in town on business, my district manager was showing me around because I'm looking for a house up this way, and he did a three-point and the bumper kissed your gate. I need to call the auto club so I can get a tow. The car won't start." Dutifully, Luther Steel tried the key several times as background effect, cutting it off just in time so it wouldn't start. "I've got an early morning flight down to Dallas. Send somebody out here and I can make arrangements to pay for the gate, and if you've got a cellular phone, I can call the auto club. I'll even pay for the damned call, all right?"

There was no response for a moment, then a different voice: "Somebody'll be down. I want all the occupants of the car to get out and stand in the light, please. These are dangerous times, you know."

Steel whispered, "You're telling me."

"Be cool," Rocky Saddler hissed. "It's going great!"

Steel looked at his own reflection in the side-view mirror as he started to open the door. "Leave the door open. Looks less like there's something to hide," Saddler advised.

Steel said nothing, thinking he might be observed. From the side of the house a black Cadillac was starting down the drive. Steel glanced into the rental car. Rocky Saddler was using a small metal hand mirror to follow what was transpiring in the driveway. He heard Saddler whisper, "Pull down once the guy approaches the gates. I'll back your play. If there's more than one, and there probably will be, nail the guy behind the wheel if you have to. Don't even nod. Think of it this way. . . . Do you want Roger Costigan to be mayor of Metro?"

Another powerful argument with inescapable logic.

The Cadillac, so black and waxed that it looked

spit-shined, stopped about fifteen feet from the gates. Luther Steel didn't want to disappoint Rocky Saddler, but nothing he had on him would reliably penetrate the apparently bullet-resistant glass of the Cadillac.

A man got out from the passenger side. The glass of the windshield was so darkly tinted, it was impossible to see the man who had to be behind the wheel.

The man who had just stepped out approached the gate. He was white, tough-looking in an odd way, dressed in short shorts and an aloha shirt, a bulge under his shirt just where it should be if he was right-handed.

"So—you fucked up this rent-a-wreck, huh?" The voice was a little higher pitched than it should be, the intonation a little feminine-sounding.

"Yeah. Messed up your gate a little too."

"You Latin or something, big guy?"

"No," Runningdeer answered honestly.

"I've got an eye for nationalities." He smiled. Steel bet himself that wasn't all the man had an eye for.

The man in the aloha shirt approached the gate nearest to Runningdeer. "Shit of a mess, huh? You okay?"

Steel prayed Runningdeer would bite. Runningdeer did. "Feeling a little faint." Runningdeer smiled.

"Maybe a glass of water or something would help. I wish I could ask you in, but the boss just gets really bitchy. Hang loose." And he smiled conspiratorially. Steel felt like he would get sick, and imagined Bill Runningdeer felt worse. "Hey—Leonard. Drive up to the house, would you, and get a carafe of water and a glass?" He turned to Bill Runningdeer. "Would you like an aspirin, maybe, or something?"

"Water'd be just great."

The man in the aloha shirt glanced toward Steel, apparently wasn't interested, then shouted back to the driver, "Water's all, Leonard,"

The Cadillac backed up, did a tight three-point, and started back along the driveway. When the man in the aloha shirt looked back at Runningdeer, Runningdeer had the Uzi out from under his raincoat. "One thing I don't like and you die. Understand?"

Aloha shirt just froze. . . .

David Holden stopped at Cindy Brown's little condo, reconnoitering around the condo's perimeter first to guard against a trap, then approaching the door. He knocked, disappeared into the bushes just in case, and waited until she opened the door. "Who is it?"

He stepped out of the bushes. "Me."

"Come in!"

Holden vaulted the small porch rail and stepped through, feeling naked in his weaponless state. But the house was empty except for Cindy and himself. She had changed, jeans and a designer T-shirt and clean white track shoes. "Did you learn anything, David?"

The furniture looked like it was the same sort of thing used in the rooms and probably was. He looked into her eyes. "You were right about those rooms. I have to get down to the helipad. But I wanted to let you know I appreciate this. And if something happens to me, just in case of that, I want to ask another favor."

"Oh, anything, David!" She pressed the palms of her hands together at chest level, just looking up at him. He put a hand on her shoulder.

"All right. I came here with a woman." Her eyes went hard for an instant. "She's a terrific fighter in the Patriots and very brave—like you. She's taken a job here as a waitress. She'll be coming over on tomorrow's ferry. She starts the breakfast shift."

"That means five o'clock." And her arms went limp at her sides.

"I want you to tell her I have all I think we can get and she should take the first ferry back. That's all you have to tell her." Rosie's planned penetration of Charlie Lang's offices might net them hard evidence, but it was too dangerous.

"Then I'm coming with you to the helipad. I've got to. And I've got this." For an instant he hoped she had a gun, but she turned to face the sofa and opened a metal case. Inside it was a video camera.

"All right." Holden smiled. . . .

When Leonard appeared at the gate, aloha shirt, whose name was Ricky, asked him to bring the carafe of water over. They looked like bookends, Steel realized when Leonard stepped out of the car. Except the patterns of their aloha shirts were different.

When Leonard came up with the water Steel brought the little 66 2½ out from under the left side of his coat. "Freeze, Leonard."

"Do as they say!" Ricky urged.

Leonard froze.

Runningdeer made his Uzi appear again and Rocky Saddler slid out from the floor of the front seat, staying to a crouch, moving to the gate on his knees, his Browning High Power pointed through the gate at Leonard and Ricky. "Hand your guns through, and one false move out of either of you, I blow both your balls off, right?"

Two .45s came through the verticals of the gate, Bill Runningdeer dropping them into his raincoat pocket, the coat sagging heavily under the weight.

"Now," Rocky ordered, "call up to the house and say you have to open the gate in order to separate it from the bumper of the car. Tell whoever's up at the house that the car can be started and driven off. Do it, Ricky."

Ricky walked hesitantly to the squawk box, pushing the button, saying exactly what Rocky had told him to say. A hard, menacing voice came back: "Do it quick. It's late."

Ricky returned to the gate.

"Open the gate, Ricky, then, Leonard, you start lifting the hood of the car here."

Ricky went to the gate controls, set into a metal box about twenty feet inside, opened the lid, and worked some buttons. The gate began opening inward. Rocky Saddler slipped through, still in a low crouch, ran forward, and flattened himself on the ground in front of the Cadillac.

Steel could hear him as he ordered. "Ricky— Leonard's fixing the car. You need to take a shit so you're going back up to the house. Tell your man on the other end of the intercom. Now. And when you back up for that turn, I'm coming in right beside you. Go talk."

"Yes, sir."

Ricky went to the squawk box. . . .

There was a rocky promontory overlooking the helipad, the helipad set off on a spit of land like a small peninsula, just beyond the golf course. David Holden and Cindy Brown lay side by side in the rocks, watching. A pilot had already come to the machine and there were occasional mechanical sounds audible in the otherwise still night air. Cindy Brown whispered to him, "I was watching the news while you were checking on the north wing. Well, there's rioting in Metro, or at least that's what they say. Voter registration records have been lost in some precincts, another election judge and his family were found killed in their homes like that horrible thing the other day. The newscaster was saying that they expect terrible violence on election day and was almost encouraging people to stay home."

David Holden said nothing, only watched the helicopter. . . .

Rose Shepherd awoke, her neck stiff, her kidneys screaming at her again. The door into her little room opened and Johnson or Borsoi or whoever he was entered, Charlie Lang beside him. Two men, handguns drawn, followed them in. "Have a pleasant stay here?" Johnson asked her.

She wanted to tell him, made muted animal sounds as she tried with the gag in her mouth, gave up.

"I promised you a ride, remember? Not a very long ride. Just about ten miles out ought to do it. Then good-bye, Detective Shepherd. I'd like to have spent the time interrogating you, but I was otherwise engaged. Last-minute plans for the election and all. The more violence there is, the better, of course. And I'm sure you'd be a great deal of fun for my men who are coming in. All those long lonely nights aboard a submarine. They could show you a good time. But there is no time for that either. So I hope you can swim with your hands tied behind your back." He smiled at her, ordering one of the men, "Get her out of the chair, keep her hands tied and her mouth gagged and throw a rope around her neck for me so she comes along like a nice girl. Be quick about it. We are running out of time." As one of the men opened a switchblade and came toward her, she noticed what Charlie Lang had under his arm. It was a ledger book, identical to the one David had taken from inside Roger Costigan's little safe.

CHAPTER 35

Luther Steel was beginning to worry. He'd seen the Cadillac disappear behind the house, then watched the house for what seemed like an eternity. No sign of Rocky Saddler. Nothing. "Maybe he got in over his head this time," Bill Runningdeer said, echoing Steel's own thoughts.

Leonard started to speak and Steel told him, "Shut up, Leonard." Leonard shut up.

Steel had just decided to go through the gate when the squawk box came alive. "Luther. Bill. Bring that other loser up here and start firing up your questions. We're home free." It was Rocky Saddler. . . .

Steel entered the house—the door was ajar—with both guns in his hands, Bill Runningdeer right behind him with the Uzi in one fist and his pistol, also a Sig-Sauer P-226, in the other. Leonard was handcuffed to the rental car's steering wheel.

The foyer was enormous, a huge crystal chandelier hanging from the ceiling at its center, surrounding the chandelier concentric circles of ornamental plaster work of the type used in Colonial mansions. The wallpaper on the flanking walls was velvet, and the meticulously tiled floor was set with an oriental rug—a genuine one—at its center.

"Luther! Come on in." Rocky Saddler's voice filtered out from beyond two wide-open oak-panel doors on the right side of the foyer.

Steel took one side of the doorway, Runningdeer

the other. "Remember. We can't lose Rocky," Steel hissed.

Runningdeer nodded.

Bill Runningdeer went through first, crossing from right to left with the submachine gun ready to fire, Steel in just after him, crossing left to right.

Luther Steel froze.

Rocky Saddler sat in a leather easy chair, heels balanced on the corner of a huge, ornately trimmed wooden desk with a leather front panel that exactly matched the easy chair. The leather was purple. The TEC-9 was in Rocky's right fist. He smoked a cigarette. "Number three for the day." He smiled, exhaling.

On the floor at his feet, as though he were caught in the midst of story hour at the library, sat six men, one of them Ricky, four of them presumably Reginald Hastings's remaining security personnel, the last man looking grossly uncomfortable.

As Steel and Runningdeer approached, guns still ready, Steel noticed darkening bruises on the face of the largest of the bodyguards, a impromptu handkerchief bandage affixed to the right temple of another of the guards with Scotch tape. Still another of the guards was in considerable pain, judging from the expression on his face, and as Steel neared the man he could see why. The mouth was a bloody mess and the man—shirtless—was using his shirt like a sponge.

The last man, most uncomfortable-looking of all of them, was grossly fat. He was naked from the waist down, from the waist up wearing a lavender nightshirt.

Rocky Saddler exhaled smoke through his nostrils as he spoke. "Reginald Hastings here promised he'd show us his records. Not the kind you listen to, of course, but the kind with appointments for his call boys and things like that."

Luther Steel looked down on the man. "Do you

have hard evidence linking Roger Costigan to your . . ." Steel couldn't think of a word.

"Escort service?" Rocky Saddler supplied. "He's got that and he's got a little record book he keeps of his cocaine acquisitions, just in case he gets bad stuff. Tell us who trades you cocaine for boys, Reginald."

Reginald Hastings started to weep, big tears, heavy sobs racking his body. Through it all he whimpered, "Roger . . . Roger Costigan."

"What does he do with the rest of his cocaine, Reginald? You can't use it all. What does he do with it, Reginald?"

"Sells . . . sells it to . . ."

"To do what?" Rocky Saddler coaxed.

"Money for the Front for the Liberation of North America. He told me that."

Luther Steel looked at his watch. It was almost tomorrow. "We can't trust the airports. We had a bad experience." He looked at Bill Runningdeer. "Get on the phone. You know to whom. Get us warrants for Reginald Hastings and Roger Costigan. Get us two carloads of people we can trust. We're driving down to Metro. If we can do it with sirens, we'll make it."

"Gosh, fellas"—Rocky Saddler grinned, stubbing out his cigarette—"does this mean good-bye?"

CHAPTER 36

It was past time for the chopper to take off. The sprinkler system for the golf course had come on, then shut off. Holden's and Cindy Brown's clothes were soaked. The video camera remained dry and in its case.

David Holden studied the face of his Rolex for a moment. It was already tomorrow. In fewer than thirty hours the polls would open and Roger Costigan would waltz in as mayor of Metro with the lightest voter turnout in the history of the city.

Holden wished he could smoke, but the light from a cigarette might be seen, and, in any event, his cigarettes were sodden.

He waited.

"Look!" Cindy Brown gasped.

David Holden looked along the golf course. Coming up over a low rise were three golf carts. There was a flash of white in one of the carts. Holden strained his eyes to see more clearly. Without looking toward the chopper he could hear the main rotor increase revolutions. Apparently the pilot's passengers had arrived.

As the golf carts turned toward the peninsula on which the chopper pad was situated, Holden could see more clearly now. One of the passengers in the center of the three carts was attired in the black dress, white apron, and cap that comprised the waitresses' uniforms for the main dining-room staff. The cap was hanging down a little on the right side of her head, but much of the face was obscured, as if the lower portion were bandaged.

167

As the carts turned onto the peninsula, Holden saw her face. "Rosie."

"And that's Charlie Lang—with the white hair. Is Rosie your—"

"My friend, yes. A lot more than that. Listen," Holden rasped, talking as quickly as he could to Cindy Brown. "I'm going out there. I have to. I'm not sure what I'm going to do yet, but I have to do something. I'm going to trust you with a telephone number. I want you to take the first ferry off the island tomorrow morning, call this number." He gave her the number, had her say it back. "Ask for a man named Clark Pietrowski. Tell him everything you can remember about tonight. Everything. Tell him everything you see here in the next few minutes and give him the video tape you'll have recorded. Whatever happens to me, you have to do this. Right?"

"All right . . . but . . ."

"Do you know how to run a powerboat?"

"Yes."

"Then don't wait for the ferry if you think you can steal one and get away sooner. You'll have to be the judge of that. You've been very brave. And you have to keep on being brave. Tell the man named Clark that you want him to have you picked up by people he can trust, then get you to safety. Don't try to pack up valuables or anything, just go. Your life's more important."

"But what about you, David?" Cindy Brown insisted, starting to cry.

"Look—I'll level with you. That woman out there. Rosie. I love her. I can't let her down. If that means— well—whatever it means." And David Holden brushed his lips against her cheek. "You'd make a great Patriot, Cindy. And don't forget that telephone number." David Holden repeated it for her once more as he pushed himself up and started down along the boundary between the rocks and the golf course, looking for the low ground. The artificial dew from the sprinkler system made the grass slippery and he fell. He picked himself up and ran on.

As Holden came out of the defile the beach road used by the carriages loomed ahead, and just beyond it, about five hundred yards to his right, the beginning of the peninsula. There was a wind blowing up, low breakers visible in their phosphorescent crests against the blackness of the sea. The golf carts were already unloading.

Holden broke into a dead run along the carriage road. If they saw him, they saw him. There was no way around it.

He could see Rosie Shepherd being dragged out of the golf cart at the center, falling to the ground, being dragged to her feet. Her cap blew off in the rising wind, her dress and apron billowing around her legs as they fought her toward the helicopter. She fell or was knocked down. Rosie was dragged to her feet again, this time offering no noticeable resistance.

Holden reached the peninsula, running onto the sand.

He could see four men besides the pilot, two of the men holding handguns, the white-haired man that Cindy Brown had pointed out as Charlie Lang and one other. Could it be Borsoi, the Russian, who used the alias Johnson when he organized the Metro gangbangers?

If the man was Borsoi, so much the better.

Holden was running.

Rosie was dragged toward the chopper, almost literally stuffed inside. Borsoi, if it was he, was handed something by Charlie Lang. One of the two men with handguns started toward the golf carts. Borsoi climbed aboard the chopper. Charlie Lang, holding his white hair against the downdraft of the rotor blades, walked to a second cart, the other gunman to the third.

As Holden quickened his pace one of two gunmen noticed him, shouted something.

The helicopter was starting to become airborne.

Holden sprinted past one of the golf carts, the second gunman reaching for him, Holden straight-arming him in the face.

"Get him!" someone shouted from behind him. Holden jumped as the helicopter slipped right, out over the sea, Holden's fists tightening on the support struts along the underside of the craft. Pistol shots rang out from below him. Holden's body jerked as he felt something tear at his right foot. His left hand slipped from its purchase. He hung there. Holden looked down, the rear half of the sole from his right track shoe shot away.

Holden would have sighed with relief that he wasn't actually hurt, but as the downdraft pummeled him and the natural movement of the helicopter shook him, he realized he was losing his grip with his right hand too.

Hopefully, Cindy Brown was catching all the action. He was going to be a star on film.

CHAPTER 37

The helicopter to which David Holden clung by one hand was similar to those used by the Navy for rescue exercises, combining undercarriage wheels and pontoons for amphibious capability, not the sort of thing normally needed by a resort like Cedar Ridge Islands. With a giant main rotor and side-mounted tail rotor, the helicopter was long-range capable and powerful. Lights flashed from the marker beacon and the tail pylon all the way aft. Holden looked forward, a face peering out of the partial chin bubble toward him. The way the interior lights struck the face, there was an evil cast to the eyes and cheekbones, almost diabolical. Borsoi. The landing light came on, Holden blinking his eyes against its brightness.

The fingers of Holden's right hand were involuntarily opening. With all the strength remaining to him, Holden clenched his fist as he arced his left arm upward, his forearm going over one of the struts. A layer of skin on the inside of his left forearm scraped away as he pushed, at last getting his elbow over the strut, carrying body weight with bone structure instead of just muscle. He loosened the grip of his right hand, the downdraft sucking at him, his right hand slapping upward and outward for the diagonal support strut leading out of the fuselage to the pontoon. His right fist closed over it and he hauled his body weight upward, straddling the starboard pontoon now.

He looked up, his eyes squinted against the downdraft. Through the open fuselage door he could see her. Rosie was trussed up on the floor, gagged, skirts

171

up to her hips, her feet kicking wildly toward Borsoi, if that was his name. There was a gun in Borsoi's hand.

Borsoi kicked Rosie. Her body collapsed in a heap beside a plush-covered passenger bench. Borsoi turned toward the open door, a look in his eye like nothing Holden had ever seen, like nothing human. Holden had both feet under him, wedged against the dorsal side of the pontoon, and he launched himself off it and across the airspace toward the fuselage door as Borsoi fired. The inside of Holden's right upper arm felt on fire for an instant as Holden's hands reached toward Borsoi. The gun discharged again, a cloud of insulation from the fuselage overhead showering down over them. Holden's left knee smashed upward, against the gun and Borsoi's gunhand wrist. The gun discharged again into the decking, Holden's mud-splotched white trouser leg blackened with powder burns.

Holden's right fist crossed Borsoi's jaw, snapping back Borsoi's head. Holden wheeled around, almost losing his balance in the wildly shifting fuselage, reverse side-kicking Borsoi in the chest. The pistol discharged again as Borsoi slammed back against the bulkhead. Holden ripped the fire extinguisher from beside the starboard fuselage door. As Borsoi leveled his gun David Holden sidestepped right and arced the fire extinguisher downward across Borsoi's wrist. The pistol tumbled from Borsoi's fingers, bounced across the decking.

Borsoi's head butted into Holden's abdomen and groin, driving Holden back, almost out through the open fuselage door. Holden caught hold of a panic handle beside the fuselage door, knee smashing upward, missing Borsoi's head, catching Borsoi square in the chest, both men half in and half out of the helicopter. The blackness of the sea, distinguishable from the night only by the upthrusting whitecaps, yawned open beneath them.

Holden's right fist crossed Borsoi's jaw again, snapping Borsoi's head back. Holden's raw knuckles bled. As Borsoi collapsed into the fuselage, Holden threw himself on him. Holden's left knee impacted Borsoi in the abdomen with the full force of his body weight behind it. Borsoi's eyes popped wide and he vomited, Holden dodging his face left just in time to avoid the spray. Borsoi rolled left as Holden's left hand grabbed Borsoi's head by the hair and snapped it against the decking.

Holden reached for the Glock pistol beside Rosie's feet.

As his hand closed over it he rolled onto his back. Borsoi was on his knees beside the fuselage door. He shouted, "Damn you, David Holden!" And Borsoi jumped to his feet and vaulted through the opening into the night.

On his knees, Holden reached toward Rosie Shepherd, a look of panic in her eyes. He pulled the gag down from over her mouth, the rag stuffed inside her mouth ripped away. She coughed, tried to speak. "You—you all right?" Holden stammered.

Rosie Shepherd nodded.

Holden stood shakily to his feet. His right arm was streaming blood, blood all over the pistol in his right hand. It was a flesh wound, a lot of blood, little injury, Holden told himself. The pistol tight in his fist, he approached the door, half expecting Borsoi to somehow reach up from the water hundreds of feet below.

He looked out.

Borsoi was gone.

David Holden slammed the fuselage door closed, calling to Rosie, "I'll untie you first chance I get. Did I tell you how cute you look?"

Holden stuck his head and the Glock simultaneously through the curtain into the cockpit. The pilot turned around and stared up at Holden and the muzzle of the 9mm. "Your choice, dead or alive. I can fly one of these. Not as well as you, I'm sure, but well enough. What's it gonna be?"

The pilot licked his lips, asked, "Where to, mister?"

"Get me about fifty miles inland to some rural airport and find me a telephone booth."

"Yes, sir."

David Holden turned back into the compartment, crossed it, dropped to his knees beside Rosie. His right hand was stiffening. As he started to untie her she kissed him. "I thought he had you when you jumped in and he fired."

"I thought he had me too." Holden smiled.

"Is there a bathroom on this thing?"

He didn't think there was.

CHAPTER 38

The ledger book Borsoi had taken from Charlie Lang and brought aboard the helicopter seemed to be in the same code as the book that David Holden had taken from the small safe at Roger Costigan's home. He examined it while Rosie used materials from the first-aid kit to dress his wounded right upper arm.

At the small airport where the helicopter landed, there were no facilities of the type Rosie so desperately required. She merely said, "The hell with it," took his little flashlight, and walked off into the bushes along the side of the single runway.

With the ropes that had bound Rosie's wrists, Holden bound the chopper pilot's wrists. "A friend of mine made a nice home movie of the beginning of this flight. Got your likeness in there too. Can you give me some interesting information that might help keep you out of jail, let alone help you avoid the death penalty for espionage and treason?" He didn't know if they still gave the death penalty for that, but it sounded good.

"You promise me?"

"What do you know about Roger Costigan? He ever take a midnight ride with you?"

"No—but I know some stuff. I do. I took him and Charlie Lang a couple of times to places on the mainland. Real fancy places. Rich people. Mr. Costigan and Mr. Lang had gifts for people sometimes. I snitched some."

"What kind of cargo did you snitch?" David Holden asked him.

"Cocaine."

Holden started to speak when he heard Rosie say from behind him, "I feel better now."

He looked at Rosie, then at the suddenly cooperative pilot. "Yeah. I feel better too."

Even though there hadn't been a bathroom, there was a telephone.

CHAPTER 39

It was 9:00 A.M. by the time the helicopter dispatched for them reached one of the small airports just north of Metro, this after a stop near the ferry landing on the mainland to retrieve Holden's and Rosie Shepherd's weapons from the trunks of their cars and to pick up Cindy Brown and her videotape. The ferry landing was under the control of a Navy SEAL team dispatched at the request of Rudolph Cerillia. Naval and Coast Guard vessels had sealed off Cedar Ridge Islands, no aircraft allowed to land or depart.

With the ledger, Cindy Brown's eyewitness testimony, and the videotape to back that up, Holden thought they had Roger Costigan.

"Who is this man?"

"Never mind that."

"He's David Holden, Agent Pietrowski, a wanted criminal!" Arthur Franklin, the United States attorney for the Metro region, took a step back, then stared at Rosie Shepherd. She was still in her waitress outfit. "And—and that's Detective Shepherd!"

"Go call Rudolph Cerillia, Mr. Franklin," Clark Pietrowski said. "Then look at the evidence."

They were using the same motel where they'd first met with Rudolph Cerillia, and while Arthur Franklin held a telephone shouting match with Cerillia, Rosie Shepherd showered and changed.

Holden was about to do the same when Franklin hung up. "I just spoke with the President. But I guess you know that. What's this about Special Agent Steel

177

driving down here with a witness willing to testify
against Roger Costigan?"

"He's been hanging around Mr. Cerillia too much,
I guess. Doesn't like airplanes anymore?" Clark Pietrowski smiled.

"Let me see the so-called evidence."

Holden took his shower. . . .

It was twenty-five minutes after one, Holden sitting there smoking a cigarette, barefoot, in his black
BDU pants, the only clothes he'd had in the trunk of
his car. Rosie was dressed similarly, her white shoulder
holster on over her black T-shirt. Arthur Franklin shut
off the VCR. He had watched the tape five times.

Rosie whispered to David Holden, "You look neat
hanging off the bottom of the helicopter, like some
movie guy or something."

"Try it sometime. It's not neat."

Arthur Franklin stood up, slowly rolling down his
shirt sleeves as he talked. "All right. You have a terrific
case against Charlie Lang, a passable case against Roger
Costigan. From what I understand from Rudolph Cerillia, the testimony and evidence Luther Steel obtained
against Costigan will support this, but most of the
evidence Steel obtained will be inadmissible in court.
The wrong judge might throw the whole thing out
because it'll be argued that the case's foundation was
illegally obtained evidence garnered without a search
warrant with no probable cause."

"How about the guy who first implicated Costigan—the guy that phoney nurse iced?" Rosie Shepherd
began.

"Deathbed testimony?"

Rosie smiled and nodded.

"From a known terrorist who didn't know he was
going to die. Nope. I wouldn't take this to court. I will
if I'm ordered to, and that would be fine, Costigan's

obviously so dirty, nobody should stand in the same room with him, but according to the law as it'll be interpreted, nothing. Sorry. Now, if you can find the Russian submarine or trawler or whatever that has been presumably bringing in these foreign nationals to the helicopter rendezvous and one of them can implicate Costigan, we might get that rolling and win."

Clark Pietrowski lit a cigarette. "What about we leak it to the newspapers?"

Arthur Franklin smiled. "Roger Costigan's supporters own the newspapers. By the time you have them convinced—if you can convince them—it'll make the morning papers. By that time a lot of people will have already voted. And a lot of people will look at it as smear tactics. They won't get past the headlines. If you want to risk a giant lawsuit from Costigan, fine, leak it. Chances are, without all the facts, the average voter'll go for Costigan anyway, thinking Gamby trumped this stuff up."

Rosie Shepherd stood up, started pacing the room barefoot, looking silly in BDU pants, T-shirt, shoulder holster, and a ponytail. "We gotta do something!"

David Holden went over to the television set. He turned it on, then opened the panel covering the picture controls at the front. He turned brightness all the way left.

There was volume, no picture. It was a soap opera, he guessed. "Lady—gentlemen. Let me introduce you to radio."

CHAPTER 40

By late afternoon there was violence everywhere. Borsoi, even though he was gone, had apparently trained his squads of gangbangers well. Polling places for the morning's election were torched, emergency polling-place facilities set up, some of these put to the flame. Indiscriminate attacks took place in neighborhoods throughout the city and in other cities throughout the country where elections were to be held, carloads of heavily armed street criminals drove through residential areas firing automatic weapons and shotguns at everything that moved, into homes, storefronts, throwing Molotov cocktails.

In some areas of Metro, fires raged out of control.

Some political commentators on television were openly encouraging voters, despite the critical election, to stay home for their own safety.

The FLNA announced to all the networks and major cable stations that anyone seen attempting to enter a polling place would be shot down. The police were telling residents that every effort would be made to ensure the safety of voters.

It was 5:00 P.M. when the engineer told Lem Parrish, "You're on."

"This is Lem Parrish and we're live. Most of you are used to Danny Ortega's rush-hour show with lots of music and traffic reports and tomorrow's weather. Tonight, with Metro's most important election in history just a few hours away, we have a live, remote broadcast for you. I'm in the countryside north of Metro. We're in a small abandoned farmhouse. Our power is from a portable gasoline generator. We're relaying this signal more than once so it cannot be easily traced. With me is David Holden, Professor David Holden, leader of the Metro Patriots. Dr. Holden has something to tell you about law-and-order candidate Roger Costigan. I was shocked. I have seen the evidence. I believe the evidence. Listen to Dr. Holden and you will too."

David Holden cleared his throat. "Thank you, Mr. Parrish. This all began when the Patriots were fortunate enough to be involved with the capture of an FLNA member named Abdul Wazil. He wasn't the usual street punk, but an actual foreign national with a long list of terrorist atrocities to his dubious credit. While under interrogation Abdul Wazil was murdered by a fifth columnist posing as a medical technician. Before Mr. Wazil's death he revealed the initial stages of an insidious plot against you, the voters of Metro. The FLNA had and still has its own candidate, one who is intricately tied to the smuggling of illegal drugs used to finance the FLNA, involved with child pornography and pedophilia to a degree that cannot be discussed on the radio, a man who will stop at nothing, not even murder, to become mayor of Metro, not to serve the people but the FLNA. That man's name, sad to say, is Roger Costigan."

CHAPTER 41

The violence increased by nightfall. The live remote broadcast was taped and rebroadcast, picked up by local and national radio and television stations, then broadcast throughout the evening, preempting local and national programming.

Roger Costigan was unavailable for comment.

There was no time for rest. David Holden and Rosie Shepherd split the Patriots into two groups, each group broken into as many patrols as numbers would allow, every man and woman from the Patriot camp who could carry a gun on the streets of Metro. Throughout the night the Patriots patrolled the residential neighborhoods, at times confronted by police who turned around and drove the other way, sometimes with a salute or nod or dip of the headlights, a temporary truce arising between individual officers and the Patriots, nothing official. Ralph Kaminsky, asked to comment on the Costigan affair, told newscasters that he had no knowledge of Costigan's guilt or innocence, but that David Holden was a terrorist and killer and that every police officer in Metro had orders to shoot the Patriots on sight.

At 2:00 A.M., Holden used a pay telephone to contact Clark Pietrowski. Luther Steel was expected in with his prisoner and his evidence before dawn and would rendezvous at the appointed spot.

The appointed spot was a Catholic elementary school that was the newly reassigned polling place for the neighborhood in which Harris Gamby officially resided. They surmised that Gamby would now be an

FLNA target and the most effective time to strike would be when he voted. He announced he would vote when the polls opened at 6:00 A.M.

Living on more cigarettes than he normally smoked in a month, cold coffee, and a stale doughnut, David Holden and a group of four Patriots continued their patrol.

There was a brief altercation with a car loaded with FLNA gangbangers, a brief, bloody firefight, one Patriot wounded, four FLNA-ers dead, their car liberated, weapons confiscated, bodies left for the police.

Holden and one other Patriot continued the patrol, the two remaining unscathed Patriots taking the wounded man to medical aid back at camp.

By 4:00 A.M., Holden could hardly see to drive and awoke his lone compatriot, switched seats, and crashed out for an hour.

If Harris Gamby were to be at the polling place by 6:00 A.M., David Holden wanted himself, Rosie Shepherd, and the other Patriots there by five. . . .

It was five-thirty.

David Holden stood in the street before St. Theodore's Elementary School. The nuns, perhaps out of defiance to the Front for the Liberation of North America, had hung red, white, and blue bunting over the entrance to the school lunchroom, where the polling place was situated. The voting machines had arrived at five-fifteen. So had the police.

The uneasy truce continued. The nuns served fresh, hot coffee to the police officers and to the Patriots.

Rosie Shepherd spent several minutes talking to the uniformed sergeant, returned, and stood by David Holden. "He says Kaminsky's gonna be here personally and will call for your arrest. He also says he's talked to the men. They won't touch arresting a Patriot until the election's over and the polls are closed. But maybe you should duck out of sight, David."

"You wouldn't, would you?" Holden said, putting his arm around her.

She leaned her head against his chest. . . .

News crews began setting up five minutes later. At five forty-five, Luther Steel, suit rumpled, face stubbled with salt-and-pepper beard, arrived. With him was an equally disheveled Bill Runningdeer.

Tom LeFleur and Randy Blumenthal were keeping the Chicago prisoner incommunicado.

Five minutes later Clark Pietrowski arrived alone. Cindy Brown was in a safe place and so was her videotape. The two ledger books had finally been cracked. Lists of real names of foreign nationals being used by the FLNA, the locations to which they were posted within the United States, and their assumed identities were now known. Already FBI units in major cities across the United States were tracking some of the men down. This was a major breakthrough.

"I stopped by and saw Anna Comacho. Still looks like she'll have a rough time of it, but she's hanging in there. She didn't sleep well and I kinda forced my way in. She was medicated a lot for the pain. I told her we were winning this one and I think she understood."

Luther Steel said nothing.

Rosie lit a cigarette.

They waited. . . .

At five minutes to six a limousine pulled up with a motorcycle escort of SWAT personnel.

Ralph Kaminsky stepped out of the limousine. When he saw David Holden he took a bullhorn from the backseat and ordered, "You men there—Metro police officers! Arrest that man at once."

None of the Metro cops stationed in front of St. Theodore's Elementary School moved.

"That is a direct order!"

Luther Steel shouted back to Kaminsky, not needing a bullhorn to be heard. "Not today, Mr. Kaminsky. If they arrest him, I'll arrest you for violating federal election laws. All of these Patriots are registered voters and residents of this district and here to exercise their constitutional rights. Since none of them is a convicted felon, these rights cannot be suspended. Their identification proving their registration and address will arrive before the polls close we hope. Obviously, they would not carry personal identification into battle."

Rosie smiled and laughed under her breath, "Bullshitter."

Ralph Kaminsky seemed about to speak. But a gray Lincoln, stretched to limousine proportions, turned the corner. It was Harris Gamby's car.

The car parked, no one left the vehicle for several seconds, then the door on the front passenger side opened and a security man stepped out. He walked toward where David Holden, Rosie Shepherd, Luther Steel, Bill Runningdeer, and Clark Pietrowski stood.

"Are you David Holden, sir?"

"Yes."

"Mr. Gamby would like a moment of your time, sir."

David Holden shrugged the H&K submachine gun behind his back on its sling, then followed the security man toward the gray, stretched Lincoln.

The rear door opened and Holden cautiously leaned inside, his right arm still a little stiff from the gunshot wound. "Professor Holden?"

Harris Gamby looked smaller than he did in his photographs.

"Yes, Mr. Gamby."

"Odd, about being an American, isn't it? I hate

everything you stand for, and you likely hate everything I stand for. But here we are, both of us interested in this election being held and the voters deciding. For that, I commend you, sir. I suppose, should I win, I should thank you for it. But I imagine we'd both consider that hypocritical, wouldn't we?"

Gamby smiled.

Holden smiled too. "Yes, I suppose we would, sir."

Gamby extended his hand. Holden took it.

David Holden turned and walked away, hearing the door slam, looking back as Harris Gamby exited his vehicle. His security people, the uniformed police, and a group of Patriots whom Rosie signaled into motion fell in around him.

Still cameras flashed. Video cameras hummed. Reporters tried bursting through the ranks of police, Patriots, and security to reach Gamby, firing questions toward him, an occasional "No comment" from Gamby heard over the babble of questions.

The mother superior of the school's adjoining convent waited at the door of the polling place. Gamby shook her hand, then walked inside.

Luther Steel whispered, "I'm glad that's half over."

David Holden looked at his Rolex when he heard the first rumble of a motorcycle. It was eight minutes after six. Already a dozen or more voters had lined up, were filtering inside.

The first bike came around the corner, then more streaming after it, a van and then another one, and another one coming.

Clark Pietrowski shouted over the increasing roar as he drew his revolver, "Betcha even money they're not here to vote!"

"Not in the usual way." David Holden nodded.

Luther Steel broke into a run toward the school,

shouting to the uniformed police, "Get inside, guard Gamby and the rest of the voters! Move it!"

Bill Runningdeer shifted back his raincoat, the Uzi appearing.

Rosie Shepherd swung her M-16 forward.

The sun winked up over the artificial horizon created by the steeple of the church that abutted the school building.

It would be a hot day, Holden thought absently as he started walking down the street, moving his H&K submachine gun forward into an assault position, working the tumbler off safe to full auto.

The lead bike stopped.

The other bikes immediately behind it stopped.

The vans formed a wedge blocking the street. Ralph Kaminsky was shouting something unintelligible through his bullhorn. Luther Steel ran up.

Rosie Shepherd and David Holden stood shoulder to shoulder.

A slimy voice called out from one of the vans over a P.A. system. "There's not gonna be a damned election!"

David Holden looked at Rosie. She smiled.

Clark Pietrowski laughed, "Go ahead, Holden."

Luther Steel murmured, "Right on!"

David Holden took a step forward, Rosie beside him, the others flanking him. Holden glanced back once as the street behind him swelled with Patriots, some of the uniformed cops, and even Kaminsky's SWAT people.

David Holden called back, "Maybe not today, maybe not tomorrow, or even the next day—but you and your people—FLNA, whatever you call yourselves—you lose."

The lead biker squirmed in his saddle.

Somebody near Holden coughed.

The sun moved rapidly upward over the church

and school and the residential homes surrounding them.

The FLNA spokesman inside one of the vans shouted over his P.A. system, "Get 'em!"

Somebody fired the first shot.

David Holden sidestepped left to block Rosie with his body as he opened fire and peeled three of the motorcycle riders into the street. Rosie fired from behind him, the M-16 roaring so close to his left ear that his head rang with the sound. Clark Pietrowski held his revolver one-handed and straight out in front of him, firing, catching one of the lead bikers and hurtling him from the saddle.

Holden emptied the H&K submachine gun, bringing down two more bikers, blowing out the front tire on a third man's machine, the motorcycle crashing into one of the vans. Holden reached his M-16 forward and flipped the selector to auto, bringing it to his shoulder, firing short bursts into the windshield of the nearest van, shattering the windshield. The van swerved wildly out of the street, bouncing the curb and crashing into the front of a house. As one of the van's occupants stepped out, a submachine gun in his hands, a woman suddenly appeared on the front porch of the house and shot him in the face with a shotgun.

Holden emptied the M-16 into the second van, letting it fall empty to his side, drawing the Desert Eagle. He thumbed back the hammer and fired, ripping one of the bikers from his machine. Holden stepped aside as the riderless motorcycle crashed past him.

His right leg took a hit and Holden stumbled forward. Rosie dropped to her knees beside him, still firing. "I'm all right!" Holden shouted, his right calf feeling as though it were on fire. Holden stabbed the Desert Eagle forward, fired, killing another one of the

men from the sidetracked van. Holden got to his feet.
He fired again, killing another biker.

Holden emptied the Desert Eagle into the second
van, the van swerving away, impacting a fire plug as it
bounced over the curb, overturned, and exploded.
Holden put his left arm around Rosie's shoulders,
drawing her close to him as the wash of heat from the
explosion passed over them.

The Desert Eagle empty, Holden holstered it,
drew both Beretta pistols. Rosie's .45 boomed beside
him. Luther Steel wrestled a man from his motorcycle,
kicked him twice in the face, grabbed up an Uzi, and
swung into the saddle as he wrestled the machine
upright. Steel charged the machine into the thickest of
the motorcycle-riding FLNA-ers.

Bill Runningdeer and Clark Pietrowski stood back
to back, Runningdeer firing his Uzi, Pietrowski closing
the cylinder of his revolver, firing point-blank into an
FLNA-er charging toward him, bringing the FLNA-er
down.

FLNA-ers were coming at them from all sides.
Holden, a pistol in each hand, fired, fired again and
again and again. Rosie stumbled, lurched against him.
"I'm all right!" But there was blood on the left side of
her neck.

Holden's pistols were empty.

An FLNA-er jumped from his motorcycle, Holden
sidestepped him and crashed the butt of the larger
Beretta down across the man's skull.

Holden rammed one of the twenty-round magazines into the larger Beretta, no time to reload the
smaller one. His left fist wrenched the Defender knife
free.

A knot of FLNA-ers closed around them.

"I love you!" Rosie Shepherd shouted to him.

He knew that. David Holden took the right side,

Rosie the left, Holden firing his pistol as he waded forward, and as he closed with them, using the knife.

He felt a searing pain across his left rib cage just below his shoulder holster, then a wash of cold over him. He stumbled but didn't fall.

He saw Rosie, her M-16 turned around, swatting with it as her attackers closed with her.

Holden's pistol was empty.

He threw himself onto the men surrounding Rosie, hammering at their skulls with the butt of his pistol, ramming the knife into every opening of flesh.

A rifle butt glanced off the side of his head where he had the small head wound from before. He sagged to his knees. As the man closed for the kill Holden straight-armed him in the crotch with his knife, letting the man fall past him.

Holden pushed a fresh magazine into the submachine gun, dropping the empty one into the street.

To his feet, firing three- and four-round bursts.

The FLNA-ers were falling back.

Rosie Shepherd limped toward him, using her rifle like a cane, her submachine gun at her side and her .45 in her right fist.

Runningdeer mounted a motorcycle and joined Steel, the left sleeve of Runningdeer's raincoat stained red with blood.

David Holden hurt all over. As he extended his left arm, folded it across Rosie's shoulders, the grazing wound along his left rib cage sent tremors through him. He closed his eyes against the light-headedness for an instant.

As he opened his eyes he looked toward the school. On the flagpole—he didn't know who had put it there—was the same emblem as the one emblazoned on the sleeve of his BDU jacket. The flag.

CHAPTER **42**

"You can't go back to the islands. The military or the Justice Department—maybe both—they'll strike there at any time."

"I know."

"Costigan lost the election. Gamby's in. He's vowed to take a no-holds-barred attitude against the FLNA. He said he saw what Americans believe in out front of the polling place yesterday morning. Maybe you should sleep now."

"No."

"I called the people you wanted called. They say Gamby will be dead within the hour. You need to rest."

"What about Costigan? He knows too much of—"

"We can't get to him."

He looked at Humphrey Hodges. It was Hodges, David Holden's old colleague at the university, whom he had called after the fisherman had found him, revived him.

"No medication. Nothing. When Harris Gamby is assassinated I want to know about it."

"Yes." Humphrey Hodges left the room.

He stared out the window. Sunlight. He closed his eyes against the brightness. . . .

Someone was shaking him. He opened his eyes. It was Hodges, always the supporter of the cause, always the spineless one. "You wanted to know. Look at the television."

He squinted his eyes to focus, the pain in his legs consuming him again.

The newsreader was saying, ". . . at three-forty-two P.M. Eastern time today. Official sources asking not to be identified indicate that the private plane that crashed into the home of Metro's recently named Mayor-elect Harris Gamby was packed with explosives, was little different than a guided missile. No trace of the pilot has yet been reported found. The explosion was so powerful that residents more than a mile away reported vibrating windows. The blast could be heard in downtown Metro." Something was handed to the newsreader from off-camera. He looked at it, looked off-camera, asked, "Is this confirmed?" Apparently it was. The man looked on the verge of tears. "It has—it has been confirmed, ladies and gentlemen—this is official, I'm told, that the bodies of Harris Gamby, his wife, Carlotta, and their two children, Richard and Denise, have been found in the wreckage of the Gamby home. I repeat—"

Dimitri Borsoi closed his eyes. He turned his head against his pillow. Somehow the pain from the fractures in his legs was now easier to bear.